Roses

Other Lothrop Books
by Barbara Cohen

Benny
The Binding of Isaac
Bitter Herbs and Honey
The Carp in the Bathtub
Gooseberries to Oranges
Here Come the Purim Players!
I Am Joseph
The Innkeeper's Daughter
King of the Seventh Grade
Molly's Pilgrim
Queen for a Day
R My Name Is Rosie
Thank You, Jackie Robinson
Yussel's Prayer

Roses

BARBARA COHEN

Decorations by John Steptoe

LOTHROP, LEE & SHEPARD BOOKS
NEW YORK

1 2 3 4 5 6 7 8 9 10

Library of Congress Cataloging in Publication Data
Cohen, Barbara.   Roses.
Summary: When her father steals a rare rose from a florist shop, Isabel is
pressed into employment there as payment to the hideously deformed owner.
I. Title. PZ7.C6595Ro 1984 [Fic] 83–23881 ISBN 0–688–02166–2

One

"ONCE UPON A TIME . . ." I began. And then I stopped. Instead of continuing, I took a bite out of an English muffin.

"Once upon a time what?" Faye asked. Faye is my stepmother.

"Oh, nothing," I mumbled, my mouth full.

"Mother, I can't stand it when she starts to say something and doesn't finish," Mimi complained. Mimi is my older sister. She is amazingly beautiful and amazingly aggravating.

"I can't stand it either," Faye agreed.

I swallowed the piece of muffin. "Once upon a time there was another topic of conversation in this house besides Mimi's wedding."

"There was?" my father queried with a laugh. "I can't remember."

"The wedding isn't tomorrow," Faye said. "We talk about a lot of things besides the wedding."

"We do? Let us enumerate what we have discussed at this breakfast table this morning." I ticked off the topics on my fingers. "The gown you ordered yesterday. The dishes and silver you're going to register for today. The invitations you're going to order tomorrow. Whether or not to invite the Wilcoxes to the wedding. I mean, the wedding is more than three months away. I can't understand why you're worrying about the Wilcoxes now. In three months the Wilcoxes could be dead. . . ."

"Izzie, what a dreadful thing to say," Faye remonstrated.

"In six months I could be dead. You say yourself we never know what's going to happen next," I reminded her.

"Izzie," Pops interjected quietly, "you know why Mimi and your mother have to concentrate on the wedding this week. Monday your mother goes back to work and Mimi goes back to school. Her break will be over, and she won't have a chance to do anything more about the wedding until she graduates."

I did know that, of course.

"By then," Faye added, "it will be much too late to order the dress and the invitations. The wedding will be upon us."

Mimi leaned back in her chair. "I think you're jealous, Izzie," she said. "That's all. For once, I'm getting the attention."

"I was only joking," I said with a sigh. "Really, I was only joking." It seemed to me that Mimi got as much attention as any single human being could possibly desire. Therefore, there may have been a little truth to what she said. "OK," I admitted. "So I am just a little bit jealous. Neil's wonderful. You really don't deserve him, Mimi. I hope I get a husband like him one day."

Mimi smiled, satisfied. "Stay away from him, Izzie. He's mine."

We were both teasing, and we both knew it. Someone like Mimi certainly doesn't have to worry about competition. First of all, she's a raving beauty— blue eyes, blond curls, dimples, a dainty little figure, the whole bit. She's brilliant to boot. She was getting her M.B.A. in financial planning, and five different firms had already offered her jobs at twenty-seven thousand dollars a year to start.

"I said I wanted a husband *like* him," I pointed out. "About ten or fifteen years from now. I am in no hurry."

"I'm glad to hear that," Pops said. "A wedding every ten or fifteen years is about all I can handle. I'm very happy that you're showing so much consideration for both this family's nerves and its purse." He leaned over and gave me a kiss on the cheek. "But then," he added softly, "you always do." He took another quick sip from his coffee cup and rose from the table.

"Will you be late, dear?" Faye asked. "I'm afraid supper will be rather catch-as-catch-can tonight. Mimi and I'll be gone all afternoon."

"Izzie could get supper," Mimi suggested.

"I will," I agreed. "But I might be late too. I'm going to spend the day trying to line up a summer job. I don't have school either, because of teachers' workshops. It's the first chance I've had to look, because up until last week I was so busy with the play."

Pops set his empty coffee cup on the table. "I'm seeing a new customer in Denford this afternoon. If all goes as I expect, forget about cooking tonight. I'm taking you all out."

"And if it doesn't?" Faye queried dryly.

"I'm taking you all out anyway," Pops grinned. "But to McDonald's."

"Hey, Pops," Mimi said, "if you're going to be in Denford you could do me a big favor. It would save Mom and me a lot of time."

"Sure," Pops said. "If I can."

"There's a really high-class florist shop in Denford, Castle Florists I think it's called. They did the flowers for Maggie Albright's wedding, and they were really gorgeous. Pick up their price list, and if they have a catalog of bouquets and arrangements, get that too."

"OK," he agreed quickly. "What's the address?"

"It's on Garden Street."

"Of course. Garden Street. Where else?"

"If you make your sale, you can buy me the biggest gloxinia they have," Faye interjected. She was not entirely joking.

"And you can buy me one of those dried flower arrangements to take back to school with me," Mimi ordered. "I need something to brighten up the apartment."

Pops nodded. "And you, Izzie?" he asked. "What can I buy for you?"

"A trip to Europe," I responded.

His eyebrows lifted.

"Don't worry." I laughed. "I'm going to buy it for myself. That's why I'm so busy looking for a job." I wanted to go to Europe the following summer, as soon as I graduated. Pops knew that already.

"But what can I buy for you today?"

"Nothing, Pops, really. I don't need anything."

"Nothing? Nothing at all?" His eyes looked unsmiling into mine.

The seriousness of his expression made me uncomfortable. I said the first thing that came into my head. "Bring me a rose."

"A rose? That's all?"

"A pink rose. A deep pink one. It's only March. I want a rose in March."

11

He nodded, seemingly satisfied. He kissed Faye, picked up his briefcase, and left the house.

Faye and Mimi were not far behind him. "Don't you want to come with us?" Mimi asked.

"No, thanks," I replied. "I really am set on this Europe thing. I can't expect Pops to foot the bill. I have to find a job."

"Oh, he'll pay for it," Mimi said. "He'll give you anything you want."

"If it's one of his rich years," Faye added.

Pops was a commodities broker. It was a chancy business. Some years we were rich; others we were poor. Faye couldn't stand the uncertainty. That's one of the reasons she worked in the interior decorating department of Hoffman Furniture. Or so she said, often enough. Actually, she liked her job. Faye didn't do much of anything she didn't want to do.

"I'm paying for it, whether he can afford it or not," I said. "It's enough that he foots the bill for college. He's no millionaire."

"That's for sure," Faye agreed.

"Look for a job tomorrow after school," Mimi suggested. "The maid of honor is supposed to help the bride pick out the stuff she needs. It's your duty."

I felt a stab of guilt. "Is it really?" I had been wondering for a while now just what it was a maid of honor was supposed to do other than hold the bride's bouquet during the wedding ceremony.

"Sure," Mimi responded. "It says so right in the bride's magazine. You want me to show you?"

"I believe you."

She giggled. "Silly. You'll believe anything. I have Mom; I certainly don't need you. You have taste where you sit anyway." I started to protest, and she held up her hand. "It's all right. It's only because you're not interested. Some day you will be, and then Mom and I will help you. You'll improve."

I couldn't conceive of the day when I'd care about silver and china patterns. In a world where millions of people starved to death this whole wedding business seemed to me a frightful waste of money. However, I knew this was not the moment to initiate a discussion of my theories concerning social responsibility. I'd wait until after the wedding for that if I didn't want to be strung up on the nearest oak tree.

"Go ahead," Mimi added magnanimously. "Look for your job. We'll see you later."

They left. After I'd loaded the dishwasher and straightened up the kitchen, I left too. I walked into every shop and restaurant on Main Street. I had absolutely no luck whatsoever. The responses I received were varied.

"We don't need anyone."

"I don't hire summer help."

"I wait for the college kids."

"I need someone with experience."

"Don't you know this country is in the middle of a recession?"

They all added up to the same thing—no job.

By noon I was exhausted. I went into Donato's for a slice of pizza and a Coke. The kids all hung out there. Maybe I'd run into some of my buddies from the drama club and cheer up.

At first I didn't see a soul I knew. I should have expected that on a school holiday. And then I noticed Rob Palowski sitting at a table with his girl friend, Helena Gruber. They were at the far end of the room. I sat down in the booth nearest the door. It's not that I didn't like them. I liked them both well enough. We ran with the same crowd, and I knew them pretty well. But they were so entirely engrossed in each other that they didn't even see me. I didn't want to intrude.

Kitty Fine brought my pizza and Coke. Like me, she was a high-school junior. Unlike me, she was fortunate enough to be among the employed.

"Does Don need any more help?" I asked her as she set my food in front of me.

Kitty shook her head. "It's been really slow," she said. "Don says it's the times. He hopes business will pick up by summer. I hope so too. Right now, tips are lousy. I hang in here because I really can't afford to be without a job, but I was thinking of looking for something else."

"Don't," I advised her. "I don't think there is anything else."

"Yeah," she agreed. "I guess things are rough everywhere."

"If I had my license," I said, "I could look for something farther away. They're always hiring at the McDonald's on the highway."

"I have my license," she said with a small laugh. "A license isn't enough. You also have to have a car. I don't make anything like enough to support a car."

"Pick up," Don called from behind the counter.

"I gotta go." Kitty hurried off, and I began to eat. A moment later Helena walked by me toward the door, her face frozen, her eyes staring straight ahead.

"Hi, Helena," I called.

If she heard me, she chose to ignore me. She walked out without a glance in my direction. I turned toward the table where she had been sitting. Rob was looking straight at me. Unlike Helena, he saw me. He rose, picked up his soda can, and came right to my table. "Hi, Izzie," he said. His forehead was drawn tight in a frown.

"Hello, Rob," I replied.

"Do you mind if I sit down with you?" he asked. "I don't feature being alone right now."

"I don't mind."

He sat down. I drew my legs back so that my knees would be in no danger of bumping his. He placed an elbow on the table and rested his chin in his hand. "Women!" he muttered with an angry shake of his head.

"Men!" I immediately retorted.

Instantly, he grinned. "You want to know what happened?" he asked.

"It's clear you want to tell me," I replied.

"She walked out on me because I told her I won't go with her tonight to her cousin's wake. I mean, I didn't know the old guy; why should I go to his wake? She doesn't want to go either. Her mother says she has to. But I don't have to. Why should I kill an evening sitting around with her boring relatives?"

"Maybe just to keep her company," I suggested.

"Well, now she says we're through."

"She'll get over it."

He grinned again. "Yeah, I know." But then he added, "Maybe I don't want her to get over it. Maybe I'm tired of this on-again, off-again stuff she puts me through for every little thing. Maybe if it were someone else's cousin's wake, I wouldn't mind going. Maybe it's time for a change, Izzie. Maybe I need someone I can really talk to, instead of someone who just plays a lot of kindergarten games."

He didn't mean it. I was sure he didn't mean it. He'd paid some attention to other girls when he and Helena were on the outs, cheerleader types like Danielle Finn and Lissa Koerner, but never for more than a few days.

"You're really crazy about Helena, Rob. Everyone knows that. And she's crazy about you. You'll be lovey-dovey again by the weekend."

He relaxed and leaned back in the booth. His long, slim fingers circled his soda can. "How come no boyfriend for you, Izzie?" he asked coolly. "You're about the best looking girl in the whole damn school."

"Don't be ridiculous."

His eyes gleamed. "No, I mean it. You seem to have a lovely disposition, you're smart, and you star in every play the drama club puts on. Isn't it about time you gave some guy a chance?"

"No one asks me," I replied dryly.

"Because you never act like you're interested," Rob said. "A girl has to send out a few signals."

I didn't reply, but I felt my cheeks grow hot.

He noticed my blush. "Maybe you're scared," he suggested.

I found my tongue. "This conversation is just a little too personal. I have to go now anyway." I stood up so Kitty would see me and bring my check.

"I'm right," he said with a lift of his eyebrows. "I know I'm right."

"You're infuriating, is what you are," I snapped.

"That may be. But I'm also right." He stood up too. "Come on, Izzie, I'll walk you."

I shook my head. "Like hell you will," I said. I plopped two dollar bills on the table and strode out of the restaurant as quickly as I could without actually running.

My afternoon was no more successful than my morning. I returned home around four o'clock, exhausted, discouraged, and annoyed. Exhausted because I'd walked ten miles. Discouraged because no one had even murmured as much as "Try again next month." Annoyed because of what Rob had said. I'd never let him know it, but he'd touched a sore spot.

There was something wrong with me, I knew. I really wasn't normal. We were well into the final quarter of the twentieth century, half the girls I knew had slept with their boyfriends, and the other half longed for a boyfriend to sleep with. At least, they longed for a boyfriend—for someone to love, someone to love them. Not me. I'd made out at parties when I was in seventh and eighth grades because everyone else did, and I'd hated it. Who needs some guy's grubby, sweaty hands and mouth all over her face and body? Most girls, obviously—but not me.

Maybe I was afraid, but I didn't think so. Mainly, I was disgusted. I really liked Neil, of course, but he was my sister's fiancé, and I couldn't even imagine making out with him. No guy interested me that way, and I was way past junior high now and didn't have to pretend anymore.

I sat at the kitchen table with a cup of tea and stared out the picture window at the fuzzy catkins of the pussy willow tree that brushed against the glass. They bloomed so early, long before anything else in the garden had even poked a leaf through the earth.

Not like me. Either I was abnormal, retarded, or stuck with a lump of ice where my heart was supposed to be. I didn't love anyone in the whole world, really, except Pops. And the funny thing was, since no one engaged my emotions, not even the kids with whom I appeared in shows, I had little difficulty behaving with perfect pleasantness to most people most of the time. That's why Rob Palowski could say I seemed to have a "lovely disposition." No one knew I had a lump of ice for a heart, except me—and maybe Rob. And I wished he didn't.

I was staring into my teacup as if I were a gypsy who could read fortunes in tea leaves, when Faye and Mimi waltzed into the house and spread catalogs and brochures out on the kitchen table to show me the china and silver patterns that Mimi had registered for. Also linens, pots and pans, small appliances, and kitchen knives. It seemed to me that they were leaving nothing to chance.

I was oohing and aahing over their various selections to the best of my ability when the bell rang. I ran to open the back door. It was Pops, a gloxinia in one arm, a dried flower arrangement in the other, and his briefcase dangling by its handle from his wrist. He must have pushed the bell button with his elbow.

I relieved him of the gloxinia. His face was pale, his eyes tired. "McDonald's for us tonight," I said with a smile. "That's OK; McDonald's is more fun than the fancy places."

"No, Izzie," he replied as he followed me into the kitchen. I set the gloxinia down in front of Faye. "I did very well today with my Denford customer. I thought I'd take you to La Truffe."

"Marvelous!" Mimi exclaimed. "I'll wear my new silk skirt. I was saving it for Saturday night, but La Truffe deserves it."

"The gloxinia is beautiful, darling," Faye said. "Thank you. I'm so glad you had a good day."

Pops sat down. "Faye, would you fix me a drink?" he said wearily. "I need one."

"In a minute, darling." She stood up. "Just let me find the right spot for this gloxinia."

"In the living room, Mother," Mimi suggested. "On the piano."

"Too much stuff on the piano already," Faye demurred as they left the kitchen.

Mimi paused in the doorway and turned her head. "Oh, yeah, Pops," she remembered. "Thanks for the flower arrangement."

I opened the liquor cabinet and fixed my father the bourbon and water he favored when he was really depressed. "What's the matter?" I asked. "Why so gloomy if you had a good day?"

"Don't you want your rose, honey?" he asked.

I set the glass before him. "You didn't forget. Thanks."

He opened his briefcase and slowly withdrew a single deep pink bud. I took it from him, put it to my nose, and inhaled its heavy sweetness. "It's gorgeous," I said. "It'll be even more gorgeous in a couple of days when it opens."

"Izzie," he said slowly, "it cost me dear."

"Pops, I'm sorry. I know roses are expensive, but I only asked for one—"

He didn't seem to hear me. "Or maybe it's you it cost dear. Or both of us."

"What are you talking about?" With the rose still in my hand, I sat down at the table across from him. I heard steps on the stairs. Faye had forgotten about Pops' drink. She and Mimi were going up to change.

Pops told me a story.

Two

"ACTUALLY," POPS BEGAN, "the man I had to see owns a paint factory on the outskirts of Denford. I called on him in his office, and he was very receptive." He smiled at the memory. It was the first smile I'd seen on his face since he'd walked in the door. "Arnold Kleiger's a millionaire ten times over, but he'd never involved himself in the commodities market before. He seems to trust me, and I have the feeling I'll do a lot of business with him in the future. Whether I do or not, he bought a lot today. I was with him for a couple of hours, and I was feeling really good when I left him."

"Pops," I interrupted gently, "why are you in such a nerve-racking business? You're up and you're down like a kid on a swing. Can't you do something else?"

He took a deep sip from his glass. "I used to love it. I loved the excitement. It was like climbing a mountain."

"But you don't love it anymore."

His smile was rueful. "At forty-five what could I do that would be as lucrative? I have an expensive family." I opened my mouth to protest, but he forestalled me. "Even you, Izzie. Even you. I know you buy your jeans and T-shirts in the army-navy store, and almost never put on anything else. A girl who looks like you can wear a potato sack. But I have to send you to an Ivy League university, don't I?"

"You don't *have* to." But I had never imagined going to any other kind of school.

"All right," he agreed. "I don't *have* to. I want to. And I want Mimi and Faye to be happy too. I want to give them what they want. You know that before she married me Faye had a pretty rotten time. She's made me happy. She's been a good mother to you girls. I owe her something."

Pops had married Faye ten years before, and from the first day she had always been decent to me. But it was Mimi who really loved her, and whom she really loved. Even in the beginning, Mimi had called her "Mother" while I never could, though Mimi was actually only twelve years younger than Faye and remembered our real mother a lot better than I did.

"Pops," I wondered, "was Mama's hair blond like Mimi's or more of a chestnut color like mine?" I had some snapshots of her in my desk drawer, but most of them were black and white. The colors in the others were faded and indistinct.

"It was exactly the same shade as yours. I've told you that before. You ask me that question at least twice a year."

"Do I? I'm sorry," I apologized. "But I can't see her face unless I look at a photograph. I have no image of her."

"You were so young." Pops' voice was gentler now. "You didn't say a word for two months after the funeral."

Somehow I remembered that. "Until Mrs. Agrin came." She had been the housekeeper Pops had hired to look after Mimi and me. She was a pink-cheeked, frizzy-haired, funny woman who had been very big on hugging and kissing and very down on self-pity, even in four-year-olds. She still sent us Christmas cards with long notes on them from the senior citizens' village in Florida where she now lived, even though she had been with us for only a little over a year. She left when I started first grade and I cried every night for what seemed like a lifetime, though I suppose it was only a week or two. From then until Pops married Faye, we must have gone through seventeen housekeepers. Most of them were nice enough, I suppose, but I certainly wasn't going to waste my energy caring about people who I knew perfectly well were going to disappear sooner rather than later.

"I think you should find other work before the commodities business totally exhausts you," I said. "If you're knocking yourself out for Faye, don't forget, you won't be any use to her if you get sick." I didn't quite have the nerve to say "If you die."

"I won't get sick," he promised.

"When you came in tonight, you looked sick." Maybe Faye and Mimi hadn't noticed, but I had.

"That had nothing to do with business. That's what I started to tell you about. Will you stop interrupting and listen?"

"Yes, Father." I laid my rose in my lap and demurely folded my hands on the table.

As he'd already mentioned, Pops felt pretty good after he left Mr. Arnold Kleiger's office. He remembered about the flowers, and asked Mr. Kleiger's secretary for directions to Castle Florists.

She drew him a little map. "If you get lost, don't worry about it," she said. "Ask anyone. Everyone in Denford knows where Castle Florists is."

"Why is that?" Pops asked.

"You'll know when you see it. It's a remarkable place."

The secretary's directions were perfect, and Pops didn't have to ask for further help. When he pulled into the parking lot, he understood what she had meant when she had said Castle Florists was remarkable. Not only the greenhouses, but the shop too was made of glass. The buildings were surrounded by a magnificently landscaped garden, blooming with daffodils and tulips. Pops didn't know much about flowers, but he knew enough to realize that those flowers had been forced, for it was far too early for them to be in bloom anywhere else in our part of New Jersey. "In June," he imagined, "this garden will be full of roses, and in the fall, chrysanthemums."

He went inside. The shop itself also looked like a greenhouse or perhaps a conservatory, the kind you see in movies of the thirties and forties about high society. The room was full of huge pots of exotic blooming bushes he couldn't begin to recognize. An elderly, taciturn man waited on him, silently handing him price lists and brochures about wedding flowers as he asked for them. "Your stuff certainly isn't cheap," Pops commented as his eyes rapidly scanned the pages.

"Our work is the best in the state," the man responded, almost angrily. "In three states. We do affairs in Philadelphia and New York City all the time."

"My wife and daughter will be glad to hear it," Pops said. "I'll bring them these lists, and if they're interested, they'll be over themselves." He handed the man one of his business cards. "I trust you'll take good care of them when they come in. Now I need some presents for them. A gloxinia, and a dried flower arrangement. I want them in really high-class pots too. None of those green plastic things."

"Take your pick," the old man said, pocketing the card.

"No," Pops demurred. "You choose. I'm completely ignorant about anything that actually comes up out of the ground. I'll trust your judgment. Just give me about fifty dollars' worth, altogether."

The old man selected a dried flower arrangement from among the large number scattered about on tables and shelves. "I'll get the gloxinia from the greenhouse," he said. "The ones back there are better."

A few minutes later, he returned to the shop, his face virtually hidden behind the half dozen deep blue, trumpet-shaped blossoms that grew from the pot he was carrying. He set it down on the counter and began to wrap it in green foil.

"How much?" Pops asked as he removed his wallet from his pocket.

The old man shook his head.

"You don't know? What do you mean, you don't know?"

"No charge," the old man replied without explanation.

"No charge?" Pops exclaimed. "Why not?"

The old man held up his hand. "Orders from the boss. He hopes you'll bring us your wedding."

"But this isn't just a couple of little daisies I've got here," Pops protested. "These are really expensive items."

The old man shrugged. "The boss said to make you a gift of whatever you'd selected. I don't question my boss."

"But suppose my wife and daughter decide not to bring you their wedding business?"

"So they don't. We're not asking you to sign any contracts. We'll survive, you can be sure."

"Well, thank you." Pops didn't know what else to say. "Thank you very much." He picked up the two containers of flowers and carried them out to the car. But once he had stashed them on the floor in the back, he remembered my rose.

He went back into the store. When he opened the door, a bell rang, but no one responded. The old man was gone. The room was empty. Pops called out. Still no one came. He thought it was an odd way to run a business. They gave away the merchandise, and then they left the shop unattended. They didn't seem too interested in making money.

And then he noticed something he hadn't seen before. If he had been aware of it earlier, it would have immediately reminded him of my rose, and perhaps none of the rest would have happened. But then again, maybe it would have, in some other way.

What Pops noticed was another one of those big pots, but in this one a bush was growing, a bush he was able to recognize. It was a rose bush, full of lovely pink flowers, in full bloom, just as they appear outdoors in early summer, except that the blossoms were a little different. They went from a deep pink on the edges to a pale yellowish-pink inside, and they were very large.

"Anybody home?" he called out. "Can I get some help here?"

He waited, but there was no reply. He called out again. Still, no one came.

Pops was tired of hanging around. The bush was laden with a hundred blooms. He couldn't imagine that one would be missed. He grasped a stem on which nodded a just-opened bud and pulled at it. It was tough, and he really had to tear at it to get it to separate from the bush. He had pulled a lot of bark from the branch before he realized that he should have looked for a pair of scissors or a clipper. The bush was damaged; it occurred to him that taking the flower had been a mistake.

But now, the blossom in his hand, it was too late. The best thing to do, it seemed, was just leave. He started toward the door.

But it was too late for that as well. He heard a door slam, and then a voice called out; a loud, deep voice. "Stop!" It was one of those voices one feels compelled to obey. Pops turned around, and then he saw the source of the voice. Overwhelmed by the figure confronting him across the room, he stood stock still by the door, his hand clutching the knob. He was totally incapable of moving a step.

It was the boss who faced him, the owner of Castle Florists. Pops had never seen anyone who looked like him, never, anywhere, not even in hospitals where he'd served as an orderly during the Korean War. There was no way to describe him, except to say that he was a monster. It was immediately apparent that he suffered from some awful birth defect, or nightmarish disease, or that he had survived a ghastly accident. Pops knew that, and knew also that he should feel pity and sorrow as he gazed at him. But all he experienced at the sight was a pure, undiluted horror.

The creature noticed Pops' reaction, and he laughed humorlessly. "I'm not pretty, am I?" he said. "But neither are you. I presented you with two of the loveliest things in my shop as gifts, and what is my reward? You attempt to steal one of my roses."

"I'll pay for it, gladly," Pops said. The flower seemed to weigh heavily in his hand, as if it were cast in bronze. "I came back to buy one, but no one was here."

"That is about the lamest excuse I have ever heard," he replied, taking another step toward Pops.

With shaking fingers, Pops removed his wallet from his pocket once again. "How much do I owe you?" He imagined the florist would really soak him for the rose, but he didn't care. He'd have happily handed over a hundred dollars just to be out of the place. And, of course, he also had to admit to himself that it had been inexcusable simply to take what he wanted.

"You've wounded the bush," the creature said.

"I'll pay for the whole bush," Pops assured him.

"It's a rare bush. It's virtually irreplaceable. Money cannot compensate for your insult. You'll have to do better than that." He was standing right next to Pops by then, and Pops felt as if a ten-foot grizzly bear was hulking over him.

Although he was scared, Pops was angry too. "What're you going to do?" he retorted. "Throw me in jail for a rose? I just wanted it for my youngest daughter." He took a twenty-dollar bill out of his wallet, walked over and dropped it on the counter. He didn't believe the fellow's line about the bush being irreplaceable, and surely twenty dollars was more than enough for even the rarest rose in the world.

Then he turned to leave. But he couldn't. The door was blocked by the florist's huge bulk. Pops prayed for another customer to walk in at just that moment, for he was convinced that someone who looked like a special effect in a horror movie was capable of almost anything. He could have knocked Pops over with his pinkie. "I don't want your money," he said. "Take it back. Send me your daughter Isabel instead."

"Are you crazy?"

He laughed again, his humorless laugh. "Perhaps. I'll give her a job. She wants a job, doesn't she?"

"How did you know that?"

"I read about her in the paper. She said she hoped she could earn enough money to go to Europe next summer. I saw her picture too, in the same article."

It was true. I had been interviewed by the entertainment editor of the Winter Hill *Gazette* the week I'd played the role of Emily in the drama club's production of *Our Town*.

"The picture caught my eye," the creature remarked. "It reminded me of someone I knew once, a long time ago. She was an actress too."

But Pops, worrying over another matter, paid scant attention to the explanation. "How did you know the girl in the paper was my daughter?"

"Isn't she?"

"Well, yes. . . ." Pops admitted. He crumpled the twenty-dollar bill up in his hand and returned it to his pocket.

"She loves flowers, doesn't she?"

Pops had to agree that I did.

"How old is she?"

"She'll be seventeen in May," Pops told him. "And all she wanted from me was a rose."

The fellow's voice was much calmer now, not nearly so tense with fury. "Send her here. I need more part-time help. As you can imagine, I don't find it easy to get people to work for me. But those who do work for me have been with me for years. They will assure you that I am absolutely harmless and that I pay them very well. Send her here. Perhaps I can use her."

"That's not possible," Pops insisted. "She doesn't drive yet. How would she get here? Her mother and I are both out working all day."

"My driver will pick her up. Monday at three-thirty. She should be home from school by three-thirty."

"Suppose she has to stay after school for a rehearsal or something? I think they're going to be doing another play," Pops improvised rapidly, knowing perfectly well that the two major productions of the year were over.

"I don't think so." He folded his thick arms across his massive chest. "Monday at three-thirty," he repeated.

At that moment Pops had only one objective, and that was to get out of that shop, and never step across its threshold again. So he said, "OK. I'll tell her. Now will you let me leave? I'm late already for my next appointment."

"I have your word that she will come?"

"Yes, yes, you have my word," he said, meanwhile reminding himself that a promise extracted under duress doesn't count.

The creature stepped aside and opened the door.

As Pops walked through it, he focused his eyes straight ahead and did not turn his head or say a word of farewell. He walked to his car as quickly as possible while trying to maintain some shred of dignity, but once behind the wheel, he dropped all pretenses and drove off at seventy miles an hour.

And now, several hours later, safe in his own kitchen, he was still afraid. I could see it in his eyes. "Pops, don't worry," I said. "I'm sure it was a really weird encounter, but it's nothing to worry about."

He let out his breath in a long sigh. "I don't know. People who are deformed like that—their minds can get all twisted too. Perhaps I'd better call the police."

"What for?" I asked. "He hasn't done anything. It's you who did something."

He blanched, but I went on. "He hasn't even threatened you. You're just jumping to conclusions. And I do need a job. Monday when that car comes for me, I'm going to go."

"You can't go," Pops said. "You can't go alone."

"Oh, Pops, come on," I cried. "What can he do to me in a florist shop with his helpers all over the place? If he has all these jobs in New York and Philadelphia and everywhere else, he must be a very well known, respected Denford businessman, no matter what he looks like. He's just going to give me some work, that's all. I'll be so grateful for the job, I won't give a damn if he's the Incredible Hulk himself."

"Wait till you see him before you say that," Pops warned gloomily. "But you won't see him," he added quickly. "You're not to go, and that's that."

"I have to go once, Pops," I begged. "At least once. You gave your word."

"What word? What word did you give?" Faye strolled into the kitchen, wearing new pants of shiny black cotton and a black blouse with a brilliant floral print. She looked as if she'd just stepped out of a page of *Vogue*. "Aren't you dressed yet?" she said when she saw me. "You'd better get a move on. I'm starved." She eyed Pops critically. "You'd better freshen up too, darling. You look tired." Then she remembered. "What did you mean, you gave your word?"

Pops told the story again, this time somewhat condensed. However, he included all the main points. Mimi came in during the recital, and she listened too. I imagine Pops thought they'd back him in his notion that I mustn't go, but if that was the case, he was wrong.

"Of course Izzie should go," Mimi urged immediately. "If she works for him, I'll bet he'll give us a discount on the wedding flowers, and then I can have all imported orchids on the tables like Maggie Albright."

"She wants a job," Faye agreed. "We're not going to send her to Europe. That's something she has to work for. And here's a ready-made opportunity. So the boss is ugly. So what? You think my boss is beautiful?"

"Oh, Faye, he's not just ugly; he's a monster," Pops insisted. "He's the stuff nightmares are made of. I'm sure it's not his fault, and you have to feel sorry for him and all that, but he's not the sort of person I want Izzie exposed to. To tell you the truth, I just don't trust him."

"Oh, Pops, you've always protected Izzie," Mimi complained. "Too much. You've protected her too much. It's a good idea for her to have a job. She needs to learn what the world and the people in it are really like."

"Besides," Faye reminded him, "you gave your word."

I stood up. "You're overruled, Pops," I exclaimed. I leaned over and kissed him on the cheek. "When that car comes Monday, I'm going. It'll be an adventure."

Before he could protest further, I walked out of the room. I'd leave him to Faye. She'd talk him into it. Besides, when had he ever not given in to me? Between the two of us, he didn't have a chance.

And then I ran up the stairs to change into something suitable for dinner at so grand an establishment as La Truffe.

Three

AT SCHOOL MONDAY, there was only one topic of discussion among the people I knew. Rob and Helena had really broken up this time. Their split had now persisted into its fifth day. It might be the real thing. They didn't even speak when they passed each other in the hall.

In the locker room after gym, Marla put herself forward as the most logical candidate for the position of Rob's next girl. "I went out with him before Helena even knew him," she said.

Sunny snorted derisively. "That was in seventh grade, and it lasted for two weeks."

"I think Rob and Helena really love each other," I offered. "They've broken up before. This rift may be a little more serious and may last a little longer, but they'll get over it."

"Oh, Izzie, what do you know? You're so naïve," Marla laughed. "Why do you think they broke up?"

"Rob told me," I replied. "Some silly thing about his not wanting to go to her cousin's wake."

"You can't believe that was the *real* reason."

"So what was the real reason?"

"Next year, when he goes away to college, he wants them both to be free to date other people. She doesn't want to date anyone else, and she wants him to promise not to either." Marla's voice dropped to a whisper, though in the din of the locker room no one but Sunny and me could have heard her anyway. "She's so mad I think she's holding out on him. The break was coming anyway. That business with the cousin is just an excuse."

"What makes you think he's going to rebound into your arms?" Sunny snapped.

" 'Cause I'm very willing." Marla smiled lazily. "You know perfectly well a guy like Rob isn't going to wait around very long. And there's nothing I'd like better than a couple of sessions in the back of his van. I mean, you've got to admit, he's absolutely number one gorgeous in this whole hick town. The whole state maybe. I used to think I was going to wait for love, but I've changed my mind. It's time to get started."

"Cripes, Marla," I protested, "you're only seven-teen."

"Only seventeen!" Marla exclaimed. "That's what I mean about you, Izzie. You're naïve. You're like out of another century."

Sunny rushed to my defense. "There are a lot of seventeen-year-old virgins around here besides you, me, and Izzie. Plenty of girls I know are waiting for love."

"And then they imagine that they're in love with any guy who pays attention to them and seems to know what he's doing!" Marla retorted. She turned to me. "Are you waiting for love, Izzie? Or are you waiting for marriage, like our moms had to?"

"I'm not waiting for anything," I said. "I just do what I want to do."

"Yeah," Sunny agreed. "Too many girls nowa-days do a lot of stuff because they think they have to. Just the opposite from our moms. Izzie's got the right idea. She'll do what she wants to do."

Marla snorted and raised her eyebrows, but she said nothing more. I didn't say anything either.

Sunny changed the subject. "You job hunting this afternoon again?" she asked.

"I've exhausted all the possibilities in this town," I replied. "I'll just go home after school, do some work." Which wasn't exactly a lie. I didn't want Sunny or Marla to ask me to go someplace with them after school, and I didn't want to tell them about my appointment at Castle Florists either. The truth of the matter was that after a whole weekend to think about it, I was a lot more nervous about the interview than I cared to let my father know. Nevertheless, I was resolved to go. Pops had given his word; I needed a job. But I didn't know if I was going to be offered a job or accept it if it was offered. So it was better to say nothing about it to my friends.

Besides, what was there to say? The whole story was so weird.

About three years before, an old college classmate of Dad's who lived in Oregon had come to visit us. His wife and child were with him. The parents were taking their son to see some big doctor in New York. The boy was so severely palsied that his legs were in braces to enable him to walk at all, and he had to wear a helmet on his head because he fell so often. He couldn't control his mouth or tongue very well, so he drooled all the time. He struggled desperately to speak, but the occasional phrases he managed to utter could be understood only by his parents. The boy was about my age, and he stared at me with sad eyes and a pathetic smile.

I knew his parents wanted me to talk to him. So did Pops and Faye. Above all, I knew that *he* wanted me to talk to him. But I couldn't do it. I couldn't even look at him. I felt terribly sorry for him; my heart ached for him, but I couldn't look at him. And I absolutely knew that I'd never be able to sit through a meal with him. So I made excuses and ran away.

They left the next morning before I came down. Afterward, Faye and Pops scolded me for my rudeness. "I never expected cruelty from you of all people," Pops said. "I guess the Traverses are used to that kind of rejection. They claimed they understood perfectly. They knew how busy you were, and all that. But I didn't understand. Ira is a very intelligent boy. You never bothered to find that out."

I accepted the reaming out in silence. It was entirely deserved. There was no excuse for the way I had behaved.

Eventually, I blocked the whole incident from my mind. But it came back to me in a surge as I lay in bed, trying to fall asleep after eating too much at La Truffe. I flushed with embarrassment at the memory. And then I reminded myself that though I had been revolted by Ira Travers, Pops had had no difficulty spending an entire evening with him. Yet Pops was so completely horrified by the owner of Castle Florists that he ran away from him as fast as he could, just as I had run from Ira. If Pops couldn't look at him, how would I? If I could not conceal my revulsion at the sight of Ira Travers, how would I conceal it at the sight of the owner of Castle Florists, who apparently looked much, much worse?

But I remained resolved to try. Marla was right.

I was naïve. Of course, Marla meant I was naïve about sex, but that wasn't what concerned me. I was naïve about the world. I was going to Castle Florists out of some of the same curiosity and restlessness that made me so eager for a summer in Europe. That was in addition to my renewed guilt at the memory of my behavior toward poor Ira Travers. I was going to try to make up for that too.

But I could not change the fact that now I was in a sweat about confronting the owner of Castle Florists. I could try to control my behavior. My feelings were another matter.

Promptly at three-thirty a long black Mercedes-Benz pulled up at the curb in front of our house. At first I didn't realize it was for me. I'd been expecting a van or a pickup truck with CASTLE FLORISTS painted on the side panels.

But the little old man dressed in chinos and a T-shirt who popped out of the car didn't look like a chauffeur. He looked like Pops' description of the fellow who had first waited on him at the shop. He scuttled up our walk as fast as a cockroach and rang the front bell. I had been watching from the living room window and had the door open in a moment.

"Isabel Courtney?" the little man asked.

"Yes," I said, after a moment's hesitation. It was seldom that I heard my real name.

"Leo sent me."

"Leo?"

"From Castle Florists."

"I'm ready." I grabbed the jacket and purse I'd left waiting for me on the hall table, and followed him out to the car. He came around to the passenger's side and opened the door for me. Then he settled himself behind the wheel and drove away.

We were halfway to Denford before his total silence forced me to speak. "This is a magnificent automobile," I said. "I've never ridden in anything so grand."

I decided to consider his grunt a reply.

"The flower business must be booming."

"Can't complain." His tone was entirely neutral. He did not glance in my direction.

"I guess Mr. Leo is very good at what he does. You all must be very good." Perhaps a little judicious flattery would loosen his tongue. "I don't know of what use I could be to him. I don't know a thing about flower arranging."

"We'll teach you what you need to know. If he decides to hire you."

"It's nice of him to send a car for me. Most prospective employers wouldn't go to that kind of trouble."

The little man shrugged. "I just work for him, girlie. I don't know what goes on inside his head."

"My name is Izzie."

But he already knew my name. He did not reply with his. He did not reply at all. The rest of the ride was passed in the same heavy silence with which it had begun.

When we pulled up behind the shop, I jumped out quickly, just managing to head off my driver as he came around the front end of the car to open my door. So much polite behavior coupled with such total lack of manners in conversation was unnerving.

We entered the main building through one of the greenhouses in the rear. We walked silently past countless tables loaded with spring plants in all stages of bloom. The air was thick with the scent of hyacinth. Moving through another opening, we came upon a small, pleasant workroom. A large refrigerator with glass doors lined one side of the room. On the other, more glass doors opened into another greenhouse, this one full of bushes and small trees in pots. Two long work tables bore the appurtenances of the florist's trade—wire, scissors, clippers, bowls, baskets, and all the various kinds of spongy materials that are used to hold flower arrangements in place.

My guide pointed to a couple of long metal lockers against the rear wall. "You can hang your jacket in there," he said. "Dilly will come in to show you what to do. She does most of the arrangements. You're hired to be her helper."

"Hired? Without an interview?" I had never heard of such a thing.

"It's a trial. Dilly will decide if you're any good or not."

"Well, what about hours, salary, stuff like that?" I didn't intend to be taken advantage of just because my father had pulled a rose off a bush.

"Five dollars an hour during the trial period. After that Leo will see. You can come after school on Monday, Tuesday, Wednesday, and Friday from four until six, Thursdays till nine, and eight hours on Saturday. We've made arrangements with a cab company to pick you up and bring you home again, no charge to you."

"That sounds OK," I replied coolly. It would not do to reveal the amazed delight I actually felt. Five dollars an hour was a virtual fortune. Most kids I knew who worked made no more than the legal minimum wage of three fifty an hour. And transportation thrown in. Working every afternoon plus eight hours on Saturdays would barely leave me time to do my homework, let alone attend drama club meetings or hang out with the other kids. But I wouldn't worry about those things now. The job was too good to be true. It would never last. I would simply earn as much as I could while I had the opportunity.

The little man started toward the door that I surmised must lead into the actual shop. Midway, he stopped and turned to me. "Dilly's a deaf-mute," he added abruptly. "She makes herself understood pretty good, but if you don't get what she's trying to tell you,

you just shake your head and she'll write it all down for you. You won't have no problem talking to her. She can read your lips."

He did not wait for any comment on my part, but disappeared through the doorway. I seemed to have stumbled into a freak show. I thought, however, that I could handle deaf and mute better than monstrous.

Dilly appeared almost immediately. She was a stout, smiling woman of indeterminate age. I'm bad at guessing ages anyway. Her unwrinkled complexion and high color made me think forty; but her gray hair, blue smock over a skirt and blouse, low-heeled black oxfords, and heavy hose made me think sixty.

She carried a pad and pencil in the pocket of her smock. She took them out and wrote, "Welcome, Isabel. I'm Dilly." Then she looked at me expectantly.

"Hi, Dilly," I ennunciated carefully, speaking much more loudly than normal. "Everyone calls me Izzie."

Her smile broadened and she nodded. She approached the refrigerator, then turned to me and beckoned. I realized I was supposed to follow her. She pointed to some white plastic pails in the bottom filled with long-stemmed blossoms and then to one of the tables. I realized I was supposed to carry the pails to the table. She disappeared into the side greenhouse and returned with an armload of fern and leafy branches.

Several green sponge oases were soaking in a sink

full of water against the back wall. She signaled me to bring two to the table. I did so, and she placed them in small, gold colored bowls. Then she made me follow each one of her slow, deliberate movements. She wired one oasis to a bowl; I wired the other oasis to a bowl in as close an imitation of her technique as I could manage. She trimmed a blossom or a green and placed it in the bowl in a certain position; I trimmed and placed another in exactly the same position. In this way we eventually completed two arrangements. We both worked slowly, Dilly because she was demonstrating and watching me, I because I didn't know what I was doing. But Dilly never lost her smile. When I made a mistake she corrected me with a patient gesture.

Dilly nodded and patted my shoulder when I was finished. Then she let me know I was to copy the arrangement again into another bowl. She did the same. But of course she completed five in the time it took me to do one, and that one with frequent correction at her hands. Yet, she did not seemed displeased. The afternoon passed so quickly it seemed over before it had begun. I had completed only three bowls entirely on my own, but Dilly wrote on her pad, "Thanks. See you tomorrow."

"Dilly," I said carefully, almost the first words I had uttered since we had started working together, "thank *you*." I hope she grasped my emphasis. "I learned a lot this afternoon. Just one thing—would you please tell me the name of the man who drove me here?" I had decided I preferred asking her than him. Her silence was full of connections. His silence was a wall.

She laughed, and it was a deep-throated pleasant sound. How odd to think she couldn't hear it. She wrote "Elton P. Mahoney" on her pad. "Don't forget the *P*. Always say *Mister* Mahoney." When I had read her message, she tore the sheet off the pad, crinkled it up, and threw it in the garbage pail.

Just in time. Mr. Mahoney came through the door, gestured for me to follow him, and walked rapidly back out the way we had come in. Again, he opened the car door for me. I made no effort at conversation on the way home. But when he pulled up at the curb in front of our house, I said, with a formal nod, "Thank you, Mr. Mahoney."

He looked at me, briefly startled. I popped out of the car before he could and ran up the front walk.

Mimi had gone back to school the night before, but Faye and my father were waiting for me. Pops hugged and kissed me as if my return was some kind of miracle. "Well, you don't look any the worse for wear," he said. "Not yet, anyway."

"Oh, darling, don't be ridiculous," Faye said. "No one's going to hurt your precious baby. He wasn't nearly so bad to look at as your father made out, was he, Izzie?"

"I didn't see him," I said. "I just went right to work. Other people showed me what to do."

Pops forehead wrinkled in puzzlement. "Maybe I was wrong," he said. "If I was, I'm glad."

"Wrong about what?" Faye queried.

Pops just shook his head.

"About what?" Faye persisted.

"About him. The monster."

"His name is Leo," I said, piqued.

"Is that a first name or a last name?" Faye wondered.

"I don't know." I turned to my father. "You're acting the way I did about that Travers boy. It isn't nice."

"The Travers boy was no threat. Your Mr. Leo is over six feet tall and weighs at least two hundred pounds."

"Darling, will you stop it?" Faye cried. "You imagine every male who lays eyes on Izzie is out to rape her."

"With her looks—" Pops began.

"Pops, please," I interrupted sharply.

"She'll never grow up if you don't let go," Faye said. "No wonder she never brings a boy home."

Was that the reason? I didn't know.

"We'll have dinner now," Faye said. "Come help me, Izzie."

I followed her into the kitchen, leaving Pops

alone in the living room with his bourbon. At dinner we talked about other things.

No one asked me how much I was being paid. I didn't tell. I was embarrassed actually. It seemed a lot of money for someone without any experience whatsoever.

Four

AFTER SUPPER, while I was struggling with the mysteries of math analysis, Marla called. I wasn't sorry to be interrupted. "Well, I started," she said.

"Started what?"

"My campaign. My 'Get Rob' campaign."

I tried to sound interested. "What did you do?"

"After school I went right down to Donato's. He was there. He was sitting in a booth with three other guys, but I didn't care. I sat down with them, and we talked and joked and just had a good time."

"And then he drove you home."

"No," she admitted. "But we touched knees under the table." With five people in a Donato's booth, there was no place for knees to go except up against

51

each other. "Our homerooms are right across the hall from each other," she continued, giggling. "I'll make sure to leave mine just as he leaves his. Watch out for us. I bet we'll be walking together."

"Well, happy hunting," I responded.

"Look," she said, "would you go to Donato's with me tomorrow after school? If I keep coming in alone, maybe it'll look too obvious."

"I can't. I'd like to, but I can't. Why don't you ask Sunny?"

"I want you. Everybody likes to sit with you."

"And they don't like to sit with Sunny?"

"Oh, they don't *dislike* it. That's not what I mean."

"What do you mean?"

"If you don't understand, I can't explain. Just come."

"I told you, I can't."

"Why not?"

I hesitated, but then I told her the truth. "I have a job. At a florist shop in Denford. I don't know how long it will last," I added quickly, "but in the meantime I'll make what I can. I need the money. You know I want to go to Europe next summer."

"Oh well," she said. "Then I guess I'll *have* to ask Sunny."

We chatted a little longer. After a bit I announced that math analysis was calling me, and we hung up. The receiver was hardly back in the cradle when the phone rang again. I picked it up.

"Hello," I said.

"Izzie?" I recognized the voice. It was Rob Palowski's.

"Yes. Hi, Rob." I thought I knew why he was calling. "You want the math analysis assignment?"

"I have the math analysis assignment," he said. "I just called to see how you are."

"See how I am?" I was so startled I must have sounded totally brainless. "I'm fine. I haven't been sick."

"I called to say hello, Izzie." He uttered each word with ironic emphasis. "To pass the time of day. To be friendly."

I played along. What else was there to do? "All right. Hello. How are you? I'm fine. The math analysis assignment is a bummer, and if I don't get back to it soon, I'll still be sweating over it at midnight."

"Five minutes on the phone with me won't kill you," he returned. "Want to meet me at Donato's after school tomorrow? I'll buy you a piece of pizza."

Donato's again. "I can't. I just started a job today. I have to go to work."

He asked me about the job, and I told him. Then he told me about his. He worked Saturdays repairing bikes at Winter Hill Wheels. After that, he gave me some good advice about doing the two toughest problems in the math homework. Then he said, "OK, Izzie. I'll see you in school tomorrow."

Of course he would see me in school. He saw me in school every day. "Sure," I said. "So long, Rob."

"Good night, Izzie. Sweet dreams." And then he hung up.

I tried to tell myself I had no idea what that call was all about, but I wasn't entirely dense. Poor Marla. She was in for more difficulty with her Get Rob campaign than she surmised. But it wasn't going to be me who stood in her way. Still, Rob was a friend of mine. I didn't intend to be rude to him either.

In gym the next day, Marla asked Sunny to go with her to Donato's after school, and Sunny said she'd be glad to. "Any luck this morning?" she asked. "Did he walk you to class after homeroom?"

Marla shook her head. "I didn't get out into the hall fast enough," she said gloomily. "I never saw him."

I leaned over to tie my shoes. I didn't want her to see my face. The reason she had not caught Rob at his homeroom door is because he'd managed to leave even before the bell rang and catch me as I came out of mine. He had walked me to my first-period class. On the way he'd looked over my math homework, for which kindness I was entirely grateful. There was no reason not to tell Marla about it. But I didn't tell her.

Her frown disappeared as she and Sunny hatched plans for after school. "We'll take a booth and ask him to join us when he comes in," Marla said. "That way I can be sure that he sits next to me. Whoever else is with him can sit on your side."

Sunny nodded her agreement. "I'll work it out even if I have to get up and go to the john and come back again," she said. "You can count on me." For someone who'd been shocked at Marla's scheming the day before, she sure was entering into the spirit of the enterprise today. She tapped me on the shoulder. "You're missing the fun, Izzie. But I'm glad you got a job. You wanted one so much."

"It'll be good as long as it lasts," I said. I still didn't really believe in it.

In math class Rob grinned at me from across the room. "Wait for me after class," he mouthed. I shook my head, pretending that in the din I had not understood him. When class was over I rushed from the room too quickly for him to catch up with me. I was distinctly uncomfortable. I didn't like the web of deception I seemed to be weaving for myself. I'd have to have it out with Rob before things went much further.

But that would have to wait. I hurried home after school to be sure I'd arrive in time for the cab that was supposed to pick me up. It appeared promptly at three-thirty. The driver, who immediately suggested I call her Harriet, was as expansive as Mr. Mahoney had been silent. In the twenty-minute ride to Castle Florists I found out she was divorced, she had three children, one was in college, the other two were married, a grandchild was on the way, she was seeing a nice man from Beasley who earned good money repairing TV sets, he wanted to marry her, the only problem was he drank too much, not that he was an alcoholic or anything like that, but her husband had been a drinker and once burned, twice shy, like they say.

Dilly's silence was a relief. Again I spent the afternoon copying flower arrangements she created. I was getting better at it. In two hours I did eight. I still did not think that justified my wage, but I decided that in time I might achieve sufficient skill to be worth five dollars an hour. I asked Dilly to instruct me in some of the principles of flower arranging. She smiled and nodded enthusiastically at my suggestion, as if it would please her to pass on what she knew, but then she noted on her pad, "When we have time."

"I'll come in early or stay later to learn," I said. "You won't have to pay me."

"I'll ask Leo," she wrote.

I still had not met him. As a matter of fact, that second day I saw no one but Dilly. Mr. Mahoney did not appear, and the other employees were hidden from my sight in the deep recesses of the many greenhouses. I had no occasion to go into the shop itself, since I entered and left the establishment by way of the same rear greenhouse that Mr. Mahoney had escorted me through the day before. But I wasn't lonesome. With an amazing thoughtfulness, Dilly brought in a radio, and I listened to the music on my favorite station while we worked. When Dilly tapped me on the shoulder and pointed to her watch to let me know that it was six o'clock, I was as surprised as I had been the day before. I was using my hands to make pretty things, I was learning something new, and I liked it all sufficiently well not to feel that the minutes were dragging.

Harriet drove me home again. She said she'd probably be driving me every day for the rest of the week. Next week might be different because she was taking a couple of days off to visit her married son in Scranton.

"The cab is hired for next week already?" I queried in surprise.

She nodded.

"They didn't just say maybe?"

"So far as I know, it's definite," Harriet replied. "I guess they could always cancel if they change their minds."

"Still, it's a good sign," I said. "Maybe they'll keep me."

"I'm sure they'll keep you, honey," Harriet assured me. "If they send a cab for you every day, they must think a lot of you. And you just a kid too. What do you do there?"

"Flower arrangements," I replied briefly.

"You'd think they could find a kid in Denford who could do the job just as well," Harriet said. "But maybe you have a special talent."

"Maybe," I said. But I didn't think so.

At home, Faye told me Rob Palowski had called. "He asked if he could come over after dinner. I told him it was certainly all right with me."

"It's not all right," I retorted quickly. "I have piles of homework."

"He said he was coming to help you with math."

Tonight's math was just more of the same kind of problem as last night's. I had grasped the method; I was able now to do it myself. Immediately, I picked up the phone and dialed his house while Faye stood staring at me. There was no answer and I had to hang up.

"Let him come over," Faye said. "Is that so terrible?"

"Why all of a sudden is he so interested in my math homework?" I asked her.

"So he likes you. What's wrong with that?" She shook her head. "You're a weird one, Izzie. Rob's a terrific kid—good-looking, smart, nice. Let him come over."

"He's in love with Helena. I know it. I don't want to be the one to catch him on the rebound. I can't stand these guys—here today, gone tomorrow."

"How do you know? You haven't gone out with one since the eighth-grade dance." Her glance engaged mine directly. "Sooner or later there has to be some other man in your life besides your father," she added sharply.

I returned her stare. "There will be—but who and when are things I'll decide."

"When I was your age I'd gone through three serious boyfriends already," Faye said. "Mimi too."

"I'm not you," I snapped. "I'm not Mimi. I'm me. Leave me alone." And I retreated upstairs to my room in order to avoid any further conversation on the subject.

But I never did reach Rob or anyone else at his house with whom I could leave a message telling him not to come. We were just finishing up our dinner when the doorbell rang.

"You get it," Faye said to me. "It's for you."

Pops looked at her quizzically.

"Rob Palowski," she said.

Then Pops looked at me quizzically.

"You and Rob can get right down to your work," Faye suggested as I rose from the table. "Your father will help me with the dishes."

Pops opened his mouth, and then he shut it again. Once more the sound of the doorbell rang through the house. "Coming, coming," I called as I walked down the hall. Patience didn't appear to be Rob's long suit. I opened the front door to see him standing there, his math book under his arm. "Hi," I said. "Come on in."

He entered and I shut the door. "I'll go up and get my book," I said.

"I'll come with you," he said. "We can work in your room."

"It'll be better if we work in the dining room," I returned immediately. "No one will bother us there. Go on in. I'll be right down."

When I came back with my book, I found him not in the dining room but in the kitchen, being charming to Faye and my father.

"Won't you have some coffee?" Faye was asking him. "Or perhaps a glass of milk with a piece of this peach tart? I got it at a Viennese bakery near where I work, and it's superb."

"I can attest to that," Pops agreed. He pushed his plate toward her. "I'll have another piece."

"No you won't," she replied sharply. "One's enough for you."

"Why do you buy it," Pops complained, "if you won't let me eat it?"

"I buy it just in case a growing boy should happen to walk through our door." The smile she bestowed on Rob was positively flirtatious.

"Let's get started, Rob," I intervened. "Otherwise we'll be at this junk all night." I pushed through the swinging door and entered the dining room. Rob followed a few moments later, carrying a piece of tart and a glass of milk. I was already seated at the table, glasses on, book open, pencil and paper laid out in front of me.

He pulled up a chair next to mine. I inched away, unnoticeably, I hoped. But he noticed. "Listen, Izzie," he said, "what's the matter with you? Do you think I have herpes? Or do you just hate me?"

"Of course I don't hate you. We've known each other since seventh grade."

He put his hand on top of mine, and the pencil I was holding clattered to the table. "That's not what I mean, and you know it."

Abruptly, I pulled my hand out from under his. "You broke up with Helena not even a week ago. I'm not interested in being your rebound girl, some kind of short-term experiment."

"For crissakes, I'm not asking you to be my girl." His fair skin was flushed, his blue eyes gave off sparks. "I'm asking you to go out with me, be friendly, be nice. I'm not married to Helena. I can do what I want."

"So can I. And I don't want to," I said firmly—but gently, because there was something I wanted to add. "Why don't you ask Marla out?"

He stared at me in amazement. "Marla? Why would I do that?"

"Don't you like her?"

"She's OK." His tone was entirely noncommittal.

I jumped in with both feet. "She likes you. Haven't you noticed?"

He nodded slowly. "Now I understand," he said

quietly. "Marla's your good buddy, she likes me, so you can't."

On the sheet of paper in front of me I began to doodle geometric renditions of squares and triangles.

"Whether you go out with me or not," he said at last, "I'll never go out with Marla. She's just not my type."

"And I am?" I began drawing bricks on the face of the triangle to turn it into an Egyptian pyramid.

"You're anybody's type," he replied softly. "Don't be afraid of me, Izzie. Please. Let's just try. Let's just go to the movies Saturday night."

I lifted my face from the paper now and looked at him directly. "I'll go to keep you company. I'll go because I'm your friend. But there'll be nothing more to it than that. I'll pay my own way."

He grinned, satisfied. "Cheap date. Nothing better."

"It's not a date." But Faye would see it as such, and at least she would be pleased.

"You can go now," I suggested. "This homework is just the same as last night's. I understand it—thanks to you," I felt in justice obliged to add.

He was not annoyed at such a summary dismissal. "OK, Izzie. I'll see you Saturday anyway. I'll pick you up at eight. You can't object to that, since you don't have a car." His jaunty air suggested he'd already won victory enough for one evening. The rest would follow, he seemed sure. He did not lack confidence. Why should he? He was handsome, bright, good-natured, and fun.

"I don't object," I said. The only other possibility was to ask Pops to drive me over as he had done in my junior-high days. Such a scene was a little too primitive even for me.

Rob left then. Faye heard the front door close and came into the front hall to catch me on my way up the stairs. "He's gone, already?"

"Yes," I said. "Actually, I understood the homework before he came."

"He didn't really come to do math."

"You're right, he didn't. He came to ask me to the movies Saturday night. I told him I'd go with him." That ought to forestall any further criticism.

It did. She sighed and smiled. "Good. You can wear the skirt and sweater I gave you for Christmas."

"Faye, no one wears anything but jeans to the movies." She opened her mouth to argue with me, but I did not stay to listen. "Good night, Faye," I said. "Say good night to Pops for me." I ran upstairs and shut the door behind me. Except to use the bathroom, I didn't come out of my room for the rest of the evening.

In the morning I called Marla before I left the house. "Let's walk to school together," I said. "I want to talk to you. I'll meet you by the Exxon station." We approached the school from different directions, and when we had something important to talk about we always arranged to meet at the Exxon station.

As soon as she saw me, Marla began chattering. "I'm glad you called. I was just going to call you. I wanted to tell you about yesterday afternoon. Sunny and I went to Donato's, and it worked out just great, just like I planned. We sat in a booth, and Rob came in with Tony and JoJo and a couple of girls, sophomores, I never did figure out their names. They were with Tony and JoJo anyway. So they all piled in the booth with Sunny and me, and Rob sat next to me. We had a lot of laughs. God, he's funny."

"Yes," I replied dryly. "He possesses every virtue." This was going to be even more difficult than I had imagined, and I'd never thought it was going to be easy.

"I called you last night to report," she continued eagerly. "I knew you must be dying of curiosity, but your mom said you were busy and couldn't come to the phone. What were you doing that was so important?"

The moment had come. "I had a visitor," I said.

"Sunny? She never told me she was going to your house last night. I'd have come too."

"It wasn't Sunny."

"Then who was it?"

"Rob."

For a second she seemed not to recognize the name. "Rob?"

"Rob Palowski."

"Why?" As my words penetrated her brain, the animation drained from her face. "Why? Why did you ask him over?"

"I didn't ask him. He just came."

"What did he want?" She had turned away from me, but I could hear the tension in her voice.

"He asked me out. He asked me to the movies Saturday night."

"And what did you say?" Each word seemed to fall out of her mouth like a stone.

"I said yes. But it's not a date. I'm paying my own—"

She didn't let me finish. "I should have known better than to think I could compete with you," she cried. "But I was dumb. I thought you were my friend."

"I am your friend. I don't want to compete with you."

"Then why did you say yes?"

I saw no way of telling her what Rob had said— that whether I went out with him or not, he would never go out with her. So I gave her the other reason. "To get Faye off my back."

"Any guy would have satisfied her. And you could have gotten any guy. The one you had to go after was the one I wanted." I think if we hadn't been in the middle of a busy street, she would have slapped my face.

"I didn't go after him," I protested. "And who says it would have done any good if I had? I don't know where you got this notion that members of the male sex are lined up in front of my door. Rob's the first guy who's asked me out in ages." Maybe the first since eighth grade.

"Because you don't want them to," Marla retorted. "That's the only reason. Or you didn't—until now." She cast one more furious glance in my direction, and then took off as fast as her legs would carry her. She was a good runner. I trotted after her for a minute or two, but when I realized that would take more breath than I had, I gave it up.

I tried to speak to her later in the locker room. She wouldn't look at me, and turned to Sunny instead. "Please tell Miss Courtney that under no circumstances will I ever, ever speak to her again. She has betrayed me."

"Marla, Marla, I don't blame you for being mad, but let Izzie explain. I'm sure there's a reason. . . ." Sunny's eyes were desperate. She was being torn in half between Marla and me.

But Marla picked up her clothes from the bench and moved to the other side of the room.

"She'll get over it eventually, I'm sure," Sunny whispered hastily to me. "She's been dreaming. It was perfectly obvious yesterday at Donato's that Rob is no more interested in her than he was in those two sophomores—or me, for that matter. He's just a nice guy, that's all—pleasant to everyone."

"You better go to her," I urged. "No point in her not speaking to both of us."

Sunny nodded and hurried away. I was sure she was right. I was sure that eventually Marla would get over her anger. The three of us had more or less palled around together since we had met in the chorus of the junior-high musical when we were in seventh grade. We'd had stormy times before, usually when one of us got a role the others had also tried out for, but we'd always weathered them. I figured that we would probably weather this one too. I wasn't really going to upset myself about it.

Five

HOWEVER, AS THE DAYS PASSED, in spite of my resolve, I did feel a little sick when I thought about Marla. I wasn't tied to her with bands of iron. I wasn't one of those kids who was miserable without a best friend. On the other hand, I didn't enjoy being cut dead in the corridors. I had assumed that the whole business of trying to trap Rob was merely a game for Marla. I hadn't thought she really cared about him. As a matter of fact, I still didn't think so. But she was as mad at me as if she did. Marla didn't make a whole lot of difference in my life, but Rob made even less. I resolved to go out with him Saturday night, explain to him then that Marla's goodwill was more important to me than his, and never go out with him again.

Between work and school, I was busy enough to succeed in banishing Marla from my mind most of the time. By the end of the week, I had seen Mr. Mahoney again on several occasions and caught glimpses of a number of other employees of Castle Florists, though they didn't speak to me, and no one introduced us. It was not that they were unfriendly. They waved at Dilly as they passed through our workroom and nodded in my direction. But they were always hurrying here or there, and never paused to chat. Anyway, one did not chat with Dilly.

I never laid eyes on the fabled Leo either. After the first couple of days, Pops didn't ask about him any more. I think he was relieved to be able to put his fears out of his mind.

I hoped Saturday would be different. Actually, I planned to make it different. I didn't mind the job; on the contrary, I was enjoying it. But it was one thing to experience two hours of silence each afternoon, sandwiched between the tidal waves of Harriet the cabbie's monologues. Even five hours on Thursday were bearable. It was something else, however, to contemplate a full eight hours of total wordlessness. If anyone walked through the workroom on Saturday, I planned to accost him or her directly and strike up a conversation.

That, however, did not prove necessary. As soon as I arrived on Saturday, Mr. Mahoney took me into the shop with him to wait on trade. For four hours I assisted him, and by then I was worn thin from rubbing up against so many people. Castle Florists on a Saturday morning seemed busier than Bloomingdale's the week before Christmas. I was glad to eat the sandwiches I had brought with me in the tranquil workroom with Dilly for company, and to spend the afternoon finishing up the bouquets for several Sunday weddings.

At five o'clock Mr. Mahoney brought my pay in a fat brown envelope that obviously contained bills instead of a check. "Am I satisfactory?" I asked. "Am I to come again next week?"

He nodded.

I nodded too, and smiled. Then I said good night to him and to Dilly. He grunted; she waved a farewell.

Harriet's boyfriend was pressing her to marry him. The night before he'd threatened to end the whole relationship if she refused to make it legal. She loved him and didn't want to lose him, but she was afraid to marry him. She was so engrossed in describing to me practically each encounter since their first meeting two years before that she pulled up to the curb in front of my house and kept right on talking. Not quite knowing what else to do, I kept on listening. It was interesting, actually, especially the parts about their sex life together, which she detailed with relish. They didn't sound very appetizing to me.

I glanced surreptitiously at my watch. It was after

six. Rob was coming at eight. I wanted to eat something and wash my hair before that. My hair was short,
but so thick and curly that blowing it dry took quite
a while. I also wanted to count my money and figure
out how much more I had to earn before I could buy
that airplane ticket to Paris. I was forced to interrupt
Harriet in the middle of one of her run-on sentences.
"Wow," I said, "that's really something. It's getting
kind of late, though, isn't it? My folks must be wondering what happened to me, and maybe you've got another passenger to pick up."

She laughed good-naturedly. "I do rattle on,
don't I? You're a good kid. Thanks for listening. I'll see
you on Monday."

I opened the door and hopped out of the cab, and
then turned back. "I don't think Walt will leave you,"
I said, "whether you marry him or not. He'd have to
be crazy."

"Well, thanks again, honey, for the kind words.
Have a good weekend."

"You too."

I had lied a little when I said my folks would
wonder what had happened to me. I knew they weren't
even home. They were meeting friends from Philadelphia at some restaurant in Bucks County. It was a long
drive and they had left early.

I spread peanut butter on a couple of slices of
bread, poured a glass of milk, and sat down at the

kitchen table. Then, at last, I tore open the sealed brown envelope. I took out the wad of ten- and twenty-dollar bills and counted them.

Then I counted them a second time, and a third. Instead of the one hundred and five dollars, less Social Security, that I had expected, the envelope contained two hundred and ten dollars with nothing taken out. I had thought five dollars an hour generous; ten dollars an hour was absurd. It must have been some kind of mistake. On Monday I'd take the money in with me and talk to Mr. Mahoney about it.

I peered inside the torn envelope once again, hoping it would contain some sort of clue, some kind of explanation, perhaps a slip of paper similar to the stubs that came with Faye's payroll checks listing the deductions and tax payments to date.

Something else was inside the envelope—another envelope, this one smaller, and cream-colored. I took it out and turned it over. It was addressed to "Isabel Courtney" in the kind of handwriting Faye was planning to pay a calligrapher two dollars an envelope to produce on Mimi's wedding invitations. Inside was a note card made of the same heavy, linenlike paper as the envelope and bearing a message:

Dear Miss Courtney,

I would very much appreciate it
if you would dine with me

Thursday, March 18, at six o'clock in the evening. Mr. Mahoney will escort you to my home, which is within walking distance of the shop. He will dine with us too. Your usual cab will return you home by nine-thirty, the same hour at which you would return if you were working.

Leo Koenig

I read the brief paragraph over four times. In spite of the ceremonial opening phrase, it was not an invitation. It was a summons. The first time I read it, I was too surprised to have any other reaction. The second time I read it, I was suspicious. Pops was right; this fellow was not to be trusted. He was after something. The ridiculously high wage he was paying me must be a bribe.

The third time I read the note, I was angry. Who did he think he was, ordering me about as if I owed him something other than an honest day's work for a day's pay? Who did he think I was, if he imagined he could control me merely with money? I had a good mind to show up at his place on Thursday night and tell him what he could do with his two hundred and ten dollars. I had a good mind to throw the bills right in his horrid face.

The fourth time I read the note, I made up my mind to accept the invitation. If I was to be honest with myself, I had to admit that I was now so consumed with curiosity about my mysterious employer that I was anxious to see him, no matter what he looked like. And I didn't see how I could come to any harm with Mr. Mahoney present, my parents aware of where I was—more or less—and a cab called for nine o'clock. I couldn't throw the money in his face if I wasn't with him. I would meet him, and then I would decide what I wanted to do.

But I made up my mind that I wouldn't say anything about the dinner invitation to Faye and Pops. They didn't expect me until nine-thirty on Thursdays anyway. Why run the risk of upsetting Pops all over again? As for Faye, she might feel that working for someone was one thing, but having dinner with him was quite another.

I put the dishes I had used in the dishwasher and ran upstairs to my room. I hid the money underneath my underwear. I thought I'd wait a while before I told Pops and Faye about that too. Certainly, I couldn't be bribed. On the other hand, there was no doubt about the fact that I'd hate giving it up.

When the doorbell rang exactly at eight, I was ready.

"Hi, Izzie," Rob greeted me as I opened the door. "Hey, you look great."

He was starting in already. "I look just the same as I always do," I retorted sharply.

He was not deterred. "You always look great."

"Look, Rob, cut it out. Cut it out, or I'm not going with you."

He sighed. "Boy, you're tough, Izzie. You're really tough. We can't talk about your looks, I know better than to make a pass, so what should we do?"

"Go to the movies, just like we planned." I walked down the front steps and headed for the van he'd parked in the driveway. "What are we going to see, anyway?"

He hurried to catch up with me. "There are three flicks at the cinema at the shopping center. I've seen two of them, and I bet you have too."

"Still *E.T.* and *Reds*? I think they've been there since Christmas."

"At least," he agreed as he helped me up the high step into the van. "Maybe since Labor Day. So that leaves us no choice. We see *Diner,* unless we want to ride all the way up the highway."

"*Diner*'s fine. Sunny loved it. So did Pops and Faye. It has to be a pretty hot movie if it could satisfy three people as far apart as they are."

"The best movies can do that, though," he commented. "Some movies are aimed deliberately at a particular audience, like all those John Belushi films. They were strictly for teenagers. But the best ones seems to eliminate the generation gap. Look at *E.T.* When I saw it, grandparents and grandchildren were sitting next to each other, and they were all crying."

We were launched into a discussion of movies, those we had liked and those we hadn't liked, and why. When we got to the theater, we were so busy talking that I didn't even realize Rob had paid for my ticket until he'd handed it to the usher. So I bought two huge containers of popcorn and four Almond Joy bars for us to share, and he didn't say anything about that either.

We agreed that the movie was good, but not great. It wasn't going to go on either of our lifetime Ten Best lists. But it made us start talking about the differences, and the similarities, between the growing up of the guys in the film and the adolescence we were experiencing at that very moment. I said maybe boys still ran in close-knit crowds like the one in the flick, but girls didn't. Rob said maybe I was just speaking for myself. He said Helena couldn't go to the bathroom without Phyllis and Marianne.

He suggested a pizza, but I said I'd rather eat ice cream. I figured I was a good deal less likely to run into Marla or any of the rest of the crowd at Howard Johnson's than at Donato's. We were still deep in conversation when we'd finished our sundaes, so we ordered coffee and sat in the booth until the place closed at midnight and the manager threw us out.

We drove home, still talking. The house was dark, except for the porch light.

I didn't know whether Faye and Pops were still out, or asleep. Rob walked with me to the door gripping my elbow tightly all the way. He didn't need to do that. I could see perfectly well because I'd turned on the porch light before I'd left.

As I pulled my key out of my purse and put it in the lock, he bent and kissed the tip of my ear. I whirled around and faced him. "No," I said. "None of that. You promised!"

"No, I didn't," he insisted, his hand now grasping my shoulder. "I didn't *promise.*"

"Well, it doesn't matter," I said. "I'm not going out with you again." Until that moment, I had been so busy talking with him about other things that I'd forgotten to deliver the little speech I had prepared. He had reminded me.

"Why not?" His arm dropped to his side, and his face collapsed into a frown. "You can't tell me you didn't have a good time tonight."

"I did," I admitted. "Still, I'm not going out with you again."

"Look," he said, "let's go inside. Let's talk about it inside."

I shook my head. "We'll talk out here. There isn't much to say. Marla's furious with me because I knew she liked you and I said I'd go out with you anyway."

"You're talking like we're in junior high," Rob protested. "We don't carry messages back and forth between each other any more. 'Alexa likes you, Rob.'

'But I like Helena, Susie.' 'You want me to tell her?' 'You can tell her if you want to.' Remember that stuff? We have to do it on our own now."

"Maybe so, Rob," I replied carefully. "But Marla is as close a friend as I've got. I'm afraid she means more to me than you do."

"Izzie, I think you're too good to be true," he said with a sigh. But then, in the next instant, he corrected himself. "No, I don't. I think you're dumb. Before, Marla was unhappy. Now, you and I are unhappy, and Marla's still going to be unhappy because I wouldn't go out with her if she were Brooke Shields and asked me herself."

Without another word, he turned away and ran down the porch steps. He didn't say good night.

I shrugged and let myself in the house. A little night light burned in the hall socket so that I could find my way upstairs. The doorway to Pops and Faye's bedroom was closed so I knew they were home too.

I smiled a little to myself as I undressed. I did like Rob. He was fun to talk to. But he was crazy if he thought I'd be unhappy not going out with him again. Maybe not crazy. Maybe just very sure of his own appeal. I had used him, perhaps unfairly, to placate Faye. Now she wouldn't bother me for a while. And I really hadn't been unfair, because he was using me too. I was just someone different with whom to pass the time, like Danielle and Lissa had been last year and the year before, a kind of vacation from Helena, with whom, I was sure, he was still in love. Marla had said that for my purpose any boy would have done. Well, for his, so would any girl.

Six

POPS PHONED MIMI AT SCHOOL Sunday night, the way he always did. After she'd spoken with him for five minutes and with Faye for fifteen, Faye turned to me and said, "She wants to talk to you now, Izzie."

"To me?" That was a first. I took the receiver from her hand. "Hi, Sis. How're you doing?"

"Fine, Iz. Working hard of course, but that's to be expected." She sounded cheerful.

"Me too. I did get that job at Castle Florists."

"Oh, great! Do you think they'll give you an employee's discount on my wedding flowers?"

"I don't know," I replied. Couldn't she think about anything but that wedding? Hadn't she covered the subject sufficiently in her lengthy conversation with

Faye? "I've only worked there a week. I'll wait until I'm a little better established to ask."

"OK." She was satisfied. "I have a question for you. I'm working on the invitation list—"

"Yeah, I know." That had been the main topic of her discussion with both Pops and Faye.

"—and I want to know who you're going to invite."

"Who I'm going to invite?"

"Yeah, your date. You should have a date for the wedding. You'll have more fun if you have a date."

"I thought the ushers—"

"No, they're all bringing their own girls. Stu's the best man, and of course he's bringing his wife." Stu was Neil's brother.

"I don't need a date. I'll have fun whether I invite someone special or not. I can dance with Uncle George. He loves to dance with me. Remember Grandma and Grandpa's golden anniversary party?"

"Uncle George is ninety-five years old."

"So what? Anyway, he's only eighty-seven."

"He could be dead by June."

"Not him. He'll make it to a hundred. He eats a lot of yogurt."

Mimi giggled. "Cripes, Izzie, how did we get on Uncle George? I can't believe the way you draw me into the nuttiest conversations. Seriously, now, I want you to invite someone to the wedding. But I have to know his name in a few weeks. We're sending out the invitations around May first."

"Mimi, please. There's no one I want to invite. I can dance with anyone. I'll have fun if I don't dance at all."

"Well, you consider it," she insisted. "You still have more than a month. I think you're wrong. You won't enjoy the reception if you don't dance, and everyone else will be paired off, except some of the older women."

"And Uncle George," I reminded her.

"We really ought to save him for the widows and the divorcées."

"He likes 'em young."

She giggled again. "Izzie, you're impossible. Just think about it."

"All right. I'll think about it."

"And let me know before the end of April. Or just tell Faye."

"OK, Mimi."

"Good night, Izzie."

"Good night, Sis." I placed the receiver back in its cradle.

"She's right, you know," Faye said. "You should bring someone to the wedding. Why don't you ask Rob?"

"After one date?" I retorted. "If you invite a person to your sister's wedding, he should be someone significant." I didn't tell her I wasn't going out with Rob again anyway. I didn't need to hear her moan and groan over that one.

"Oh, well, there's time," she replied. "Maybe by the end of April he will be significant."

"Leave her alone, Faye," Pops interrupted. "Let her do what she wants."

"By the end of April, Rob will be back with Helena," I said. "I'm amazed he's kept away from her this long."

"Maybe because he's interested in someone else," Faye suggested with deceptive mildness.

"Don't count on it," I called as I walked out of the room. Then I went upstairs and watched a rerun of *Brideshead Revisited* on TV. After it was over, I phoned Marla. She hung up as soon as she heard my voice. So then I phoned Sunny and told her to tell Marla I'd told Rob I wouldn't go out with him again. Rob was right. The whole thing absurdly resembled a junior-high intrigue.

In school I tried to talk to Marla, but she still turned away from me. Sunny had done as I'd asked. "But Marla's mad at you anyway," Sunny said. "She thinks that somehow it's your fault she isn't getting anywhere with Rob."

"That's ridiculous," I said. "It's even more ridiculous now."

"It isn't what you *do,* exactly," Sunny said sadly.

"I can't help existing," I returned with some asperity. "I don't plan to lie down and die for Marla's benefit."

The next day Corky Benedetti stopped me in the hall. He'd missed English because of an orthodontist appointment and wanted to know the assignment. Rob was with him. Then Corky, Rob, and I walked to math class together, Corky on one side of me, Rob on the other. If Marla was going to be mad at me regardless, I figured what the hell. Anyway, the conversation among the three of us was entirely impersonal. Rob didn't say a word about anything that had transpired Saturday night, and of course I hadn't expected him to.

The rest of the week my mind was pretty much occupied with my Thursday evening dinner engagement. I worked out about seven different scenarios for the occasion in my head. In one of them I did indeed dramatically toss two hundred and ten dollars in Mr. Leo Koenig's face. But after all, on Monday I hadn't asked Mr. Mahoney if a mistake had been made about my pay. I had decided to take that matter up directly with the big boss.

I found myself, for just about the first time in my life, worrying about what I should wear. The note had certainly suggested a degree of formality for which my usual blue jeans seemed entirely unsuitable. On the other hand, it would be silly to spend the afternoon working in a skirt. To carry a change of clothes over in a plastic cleaner's bag seemed to place too great an importance upon the occasion. In the end I achieved what I hoped was a reasonable compromise. I wore a pair of designer jeans Mimi had fortuitously left behind because they no longer fulfilled her exacting requirements, and a pretty embroidered peasant blouse Pops and Faye had given me, a present from their vacation in Mexico the year before.

Dilly noticed. "You look pretty," she wrote on her pad as soon as she saw me. "Always pretty," she scrawled hastily. "Today more so."

"Thanks," I said slowly. I always spoke slowly to Dilly and pronounced my words carefully so she wouldn't have any difficulty reading my lips. She did seem to understand me perfectly most of the time. "I thought I'd better dress a little. Mr. Koenig invited me for dinner."

A look of utter amazement crossed Dilly's face, and then one of puzzlement, as if she doubted she had understood me. "Leo?" she wrote on her pad. "The boss?"

I nodded.

"Why?" she wrote.

"I thought maybe you'd be able to tell me," I said.

She shook her head, apparently even more mystified than I was.

"Here, I'll show you the note he sent me." I took it out of my pocket and handed it to her. "Not exactly an invitation," I said when she looked up from reading it. "More like a summons. Frankly, I was tempted to say no, but this is a fantastic job and, well . . . I don't want to risk losing it unless I really have to."

Dilly nodded. She understood what I was saying.

"Do you know him?" I asked.

"Not well," she scrawled. "Been wonderful to me. Hard for me to find job. Taught me everything himself. Heard about his looks?"

"Yes," I said.

"After while, I stopped noticing so much. Awful shock at first."

My palms began to sweat as remembered fear and disgust swept over me. "Like someone with really severe palsy?"

She shook her head. "Not born that way," she wrote. "Accident."

I don't know how much good I was to Dilly for the rest of the afternoon. Things either stuck to my hands or dropped out of my fingers onto the floor. I was clumsier than I had been the first day. But Dilly didn't mention it. I suppose she understood that I was nervous.

At six o'clock I went into the john, washed my hands and face, and ran a comb through my hair. Then I walked out into the shop to find Mr. Mahoney. He was locking the front door. "We'll go out through the back," he said.

"Do you know why Mr. Koenig invited me for supper?" I ventured.

Mr. Mahoney's face was expressionless. "No," he answered shortly. He clamped his mouth shut so firmly I knew there was no point in further questions.

I followed him out through the workroom and the rear greenhouse. Behind us he locked each door we passed through. Then we walked through the gracefully landscaped garden that surrounded the shop. Beyond it lay a hedge too high to see over, too thick to see through. "We'll take the shortcut," Mr. Mahoney said, "if you don't mind. So we don't have to walk all the way around the block. It's a very big block." It was the most he had ever said to me at one time.

"I don't mind."

An opening had been made in the hedges, so narrow that Mr. Mahoney and I had to turn sideways to get through. We entered a garden similar to the one that surrounded the shop, but larger and perhaps more elaborately landscaped, though I couldn't see much detail in the thickening twilight. A large house loomed ahead, distinctly Victorian in design, surrounded on all four sides by a deep porch, and topped with a black mansard roof. The building appeared to be built of a pale sandstone, and some of its mullioned windows were filled with stained glass panes.

"We'll go around to the front," Mr. Mahoney

said. "Company's supposed to come through the front door."

"Even if they snuck through the hedge," I commented.

He uttered a snort that I took to be his version of a laugh.

We approached the wide front steps. A long brick walk led away from them, down to a high gate made out of spiked black cast iron posts that swung between two tall stone pillars. It was closed, but because of the distance and the gathering dusk, I couldn't tell whether or not it was locked. Abutting the pillars were thick hedges at least fifteen feet tall that must have rendered the house almost invisible from the street.

The porch light was on, revealing furniture of white wicker with yellow cushions, shrouded in clear plastic covers, for it was still too early in the season to sit outside. Mr. Mahoney didn't ring the bell, but opened the door with yet another one of the keys on the huge ring he carried on a leather strap attached to his belt.

We entered a wide, graceful hallway in which a long stairway with a carved mahogany banister curved its way upstairs. The floor was tiled in large black-and-white squares, gold-and-white wallpaper covered the walls, and pinpoints of light gleamed from the great brass chandelier. A huge copper bowl filled with tulips, daffodils, and iris stood on a cherry drop-leaf table against the wall. Faye said a mirror in the front hall was a principle of decorating, so guests could check themselves on the way in and residents could check themselves on the way out. I expected a mirror above the drop-leaf table. But there was none.

Mr. Mahoney opened a closet door. "I'll take your jacket," he said. I slipped it off and handed it to him.

He was hanging it up when a voice called from another room, "In the library, Mr. Mahoney." It was a rich, full baritone, echoing with implicit authority.

Mr. Mahoney and I walked down to the end of the hall and through an archway into a room lined with books and filled with highly polished old furniture. A fire burned in a fireplace edged with blue-and-white Dutch tiles, and light glimmered softly from lamps on the tables. In front of the fireplace a high-back wing chair was turned away from the entryway so it was not possible to see the face of the man who was sitting in it.

"Good evening, Mr. Mahoney," said the man in the chair. The rich baritone voice was his.

"Well, Leo, I brought her. Like you said," Mr. Mahoney replied. "I'll go now."

"No, Mr. Mahoney," Leo countered firmly, "you'll have dinner with us. Like I said."

"Leo, you know I got an ulcer," he grumbled. "If I eat those fancy sauces and drink those French wines you go for, I'll be sick for a week."

"You can have cottage cheese and a soft-boiled egg. Mrs. Mangarelli knows all about your ulcer."

"Yeah, that's what I was afraid of." With an air of resignation he sat down in a Windsor chair, picked up a copy of *National Geographic* from the table next to him, and began thumbing through it.

At the same moment, the man in the chair stood up. He was tall, as much as two heads taller than the mantelpiece. His shoulders and chest were so broad they seemed to fill the hearth, blocking, for the moment, my view of the fire. "Good evening, Isabel," he said.

"Good evening, Mr. Koenig," I replied as heartily as I could manage. "You can call me Izzie. Everybody does."

"If you don't mind, I'll stick to Isabel. It suits you better. But you can call me Leo. Everybody does." As he spoke, he moved toward me. When the light from the lamp on Mr. Mahoney's table revealed him fully, he stood still.

In spite of all my resolves, a shiver coursed its way from the base of my neck to the tip of my spine. I clenched my fists tightly enough to feel my nails dig into my palms. I had to do that to keep from turning and walking—no, running—out of the room.

He wore his thick, honey-color hair down to his shoulders in what was perhaps an effort to obscure or distract from his face. The effort failed, for the deformity of that face was totally riveting. I didn't want to look at it, but I had to look at it, just as I had to look at one of those scenes in a horror movie that I always watched through my fingers, but watched nevertheless.

Where he should have had a nose, there was only a hole. Where he should have had a mouth, there was only another hole. No eyebrows shaded his lashless black eyes, which were set like two lumps of coal in deep sockets. The skin on his face and the back of his hands was lumpy and scarred, blotches of the palest white alternating with slashes and pouches that appeared painfully inflamed. An accident, Dilly had said. He looked as if he'd walked through fire.

The hole that was his mouth moved. "I'm no beauty, am I, Isabel? Unlike you. I regret the shock. I thought your father would have prepared you."

So in spite of all my efforts at control, he had noticed my disgust. Well, I was sure it had shown in my face, and of course he would be extremely sensitive to it. "I'm sorry," I murmured. "I couldn't help it."

"Of course not," he returned quietly. "It's only natural. I guess there is no preparation. Perhaps in time you won't notice my face so much. My able assistant is accustomed to me—almost. Isn't that correct, Mr. Mahoney?"

At the sound of his name Mr. Mahoney looked up from his magazine, nodded unsmilingly, and immediately returned his eyes again to the page.

It was a relief that he had raised the issue directly. It made it easier not to have to pretend. "Sit down, please," he invited, gesturing to a chair near the one he'd been sitting in. I perceived none of the preemptory quality I had noticed in the invitation that had been enclosed in my pay envelope. His tone and his manner were entirely courteous in an old-fashioned way. Between his manners and the décor of his enormous establishment, I felt as if I had stumbled into one of the illustrations in the century-old fairy tale books they keep behind glass doors in the Winter Hill Public Library.

I acceded to his request, and he resumed the position that we had found him in when we had entered the room. My chair was placed in relation to his so that only his profile was presented to me, and it was obscured by his hair in a way that his full face could not be. I was able to sit and speak with him almost normally. But not quite. I still felt my stomach quivering, and I still had to force my voice to its normal volume and tone.

"I wanted to tell you," he said, "that your work is entirely satisfactory. We hope that you will stay with us a long time."

Had he invited me to dinner just to say that? He could have told me that in the shop, or had Mr. Mahoney or Dilly tell me, as they had told me everything else I'd needed to know.

He rang a crystal bell on the table beside him. An

elderly white-haired woman in a blue dress with an apron over it appeared. "My housekeeper, Mrs. Mangarelli," Leo said. "Mrs. Mangarelli, this is our newest employee, Isabel Courtney."

Mrs. Mangarelli nodded but did not speak as she set a tray of hot hors d'oeuvres down on the coffee table in front of me. I wondered if, like Dilly, she was deaf and mute.

"Please help yourself, Isabel," Leo said. "I can assure you everything is delicious. Mrs. Mangarelli is a superb cook." She didn't respond to his compliment, but left the room as quietly as she had entered it. "Mr. Mahoney," Leo called, "fix yourself a drink."

"You know I shouldn't drink," he complained. But he got up anyway and opened a cabinet under one of the bookshelves, revealing a small refrigerator, a miniature sink, and an elaborate array of bottles and glasses.

"Will you have something, Isabel?" Leo asked. "Mr. Mahoney will get it for you. A little wine, perhaps, or an apéritif?"

"Do you . . . would you . . . is it all right if I have a Coke?" The request sounded so absurd to me in that setting that I actually giggled.

"Of course," Leo replied with the utmost seriousness. "Mr. Mahoney, please bring Isabel a Coke."

"A Coke?" Mr. Mahoney questioned. "I never saw a can of soda in this cabinet."

"I was farsighted, Mr. Mahoney," Leo replied. "I

made sure Mrs. Mangarelli stocked up in advance for this occasion."

Mr. Mahoney rummaged about and discovered not a can but a bottle of Coca-Cola. He poured it over ice in a cut-glass tumbler and brought it to me. He seized a handful of hors d'oeuvres and carried them back to his seat with the whiskey and water he had fixed for himself. "Please, Isabel," Leo urged, "try the stuffed mushrooms. They're Mrs. Mangarelli's specialty."

I was not in the least hungry, but I politely picked one off the plate and popped it in my mouth. Mr. Mahoney was chewing away steadily. "It is very delicious," I said. I pushed the plate in Mr. Koenig's direction.

He reached out and pushed it back toward me. It was then I noticed that he had only a thumb and two fingers on his hand, and that the thumb was as long as the fingers. The three digits were bent so that his hand looked like a claw. "These are for you and Mr. Mahoney," he said. "I already ate."

"You already ate?" I echoed in surprise.

"Isabel, you would not be charmed by the sight of me consuming a meal. The lack of lips does not make it a very appetizing spectacle. It's best for all if I dine alone."

"Don't your guests find that odd?" I queried.

"I never have guests," he replied.

"Mr. Mahoney . . ."

"He doesn't count."

"I'm a guest," I reminded him.

"The first since . . ." his voice trailed off.

"Since when?"

"In a long time." He stared silently into the fire.

It was my turn. "Your house is beautiful—like something out of *Better Homes and Gardens.*"

"It's my palace," he returned quietly. "My palace, and my prison."

"You don't go out? You don't travel or anything?" If he didn't, it wasn't for lack of money.

"Of course not. You can surely understand why I must avoid strangers."

"But the business . . . Was it in your family?"

"No, I built the business. But we always had beautiful gardens, and talented people to take care of them. I learned from them."

"Surely you have to see people in the way of business?"

"I don't wait on trade, Isabel. I wouldn't have much if I did. A big part of my business is wholesale anyway. I have a refrigerated warehouse in the city, with managers and salespeople and all the rest of it. Thank God for the telephone. There's nothing wrong with my voice."

His voice was beautiful. And in spite of the lack of lips, he seemed to have no difficulty pronouncing words correctly.

"Are you happy with us, Isabel?" he asked.

"It's a good job, Mr. Koenig," I replied slowly.

"Leo," he reminded me.

"All right, Leo. A very good job." Now was the time to bring up the money. "Too good. Unless someone made a big mistake."

"What do you mean?"

"I'm not worth ten dollars an hour. I'm an inexperienced kid. None of my friends with jobs make more than five dollars. Most of them make three fifty."

"Just because the fast-food emporiums pay starvation wages doesn't mean I should join the ranks of the exploiters," he retorted. "Dilly told me you're extremely talented. An experienced florist would cost me fifteen dollars an hour. I'm saving money on you."

I wondered if that was true. I wondered if experienced florists really did make fifteen dollars an hour. Maybe he was just trying to make up for the frightful shock he'd inflicted upon my father. "Well, I can use the money," I admitted. "I'm saving for a trip to Europe next summer."

"Where in Europe were you planning to go?" He sounded as if he really wanted to know my answer.

"Everywhere!" I responded quickly.

"But in one summer you can't go everywhere. Everywhere turns out to be nowhere. You must make choices."

"I know. But how?"

He began then to speak about London, Paris,

Rome, Madrid, and the Greek islands, and of more out-of-the-way places too, like Zagreb and Transylvania and the Algarve. Though he no longer traveled, once he had roamed the world, and he seemed to remember everything he'd ever seen.

We adjourned to the dining room, and between mouthfuls of fettucini alfredo and artichokes, I plied him with questions. Mr. Mahoney was silent throughout the meal, completely ignoring the eggs and cottage cheese Mrs. Mangarelli had placed before him and stuffing himself with the goodies from the bowls that had been set in front of me. Since Leo wasn't eating, he answered my questions at length. The dining room was lit only by candles on the table that concealed as much as they illuminated. His seat at the far end was obscured by shadows. I could scarcely see him as he spoke.

After dinner we returned to his study. Mr. Mahoney again asked for permission to depart, and it was again denied. He busied himself once more with the *National Geographic,* though I suspected he was paying much more attention to our conversation than he let on. When Leo rose to get some photo albums of his travels for me to look at, Mr. Mahoney leaped up and retrieved them before Leo had taken two steps.

Outside, several long blasts of an automobile horn shattered the night's stillness. With a start, I looked up from a photograph of a long white beach along the Red Sea.

"Your taxi," Leo said.

"It's nine o'clock already?" I glanced at my watch. It was a quarter after.

"They're late," Leo said. "Speak to the driver about that, Mr. Mahoney. I don't want to incur Mr. Courtney's anger. I want Isabel to come again. You will come, Isabel, won't you?"

"Yes, Leo, I'll come again." Indeed I would. I had perhaps discovered more in one evening with Leo Koenig than I'd learned in ten years of public school social studies lessons.

"Speak to the driver, Mr. Mahoney," Leo repeated. Occasionally in his manner to Mr. Mahoney, though scarcely ever in his manner to me, I glimpsed the autocrat who'd summoned me in the curt little note. Mr. Mahoney obeyed.

"I'll walk you to the door," Leo said. In the bright light of the hall's chandelier, his inhuman face was completely visible. I looked, and then I did not look any more. My eyes were fixed straight ahead as I walked to the front door.

When we reached it Leo stretched out his claw-like hand. But then, without turning the knob, his arm dropped again to his side.

He turned to me. "Isabel," he said very quietly, almost humbly, "I will ask a favor of you. A great favor."

"What is it?" He had been lovely to me. I would comply if I could.

"Isabel, will you kiss me good night?" I had to strain to catch his words, but there was no doubt as to what he had said. I had heard him correctly.

As when I had first seen him, I shivered.

Perhaps I shivered out of disgust. I know I didn't shiver out of fear. I wasn't afraid of him. After spending an entire evening talking to him, I couldn't be afraid of him. On the other hand, I knew that he had asked something of me that I could not grant. "No, Leo," I said in a voice as quiet as his. "I can't let you do that. I just can't."

He nodded, unsurprised. "But you will come again?"

"Yes, I'll come again."

He opened the door, and I stepped out on the front porch. Lights on the stone gateposts and the porch illuminated the front walk. I couldn't see the cab waiting in the street, but impatiently the driver honked again. It probably wasn't Harriet.

I ran down the steps and hurried along the path. "Good night," Leo called.

I turned to see him standing in the doorway, fully visible in the light. He waved. So did I.

"Good night, Leo," I said. "Sleep well."

Seven

"IZZIE, IS THAT YOU?" Pops' voice called to me from the bedroom as soon as I had shut the front door behind me. He must have heard it slam.

"Who else?" I called back.

"Come on up."

He and Faye were watching TV, but when I walked in, Pops pushed the remote control button from the chair in which he was sitting and turned off the machine. "You OK?" he asked.

"Look at her," Faye said. "You can tell she's OK."

"Pops," I said, "you have Mr. Koenig all wrong. Today I finally got to meet him. He's unbearable to look at, I admit, but he was as nice to me as anyone has ever been. Courteous, considerate—"

"Brave, clean, and reverent," Pops interjected. "All of a sudden, he's a Boy Scout."

"I saw his house," I said.

"You were in his house?" Pops' eyes widened in a kind of horror. "Was he there?"

"Yes. That's when I saw him." The closer I came to telling the truth, the less danger I would be of slipping up one day. But I could see from Pops' expression that I didn't dare tell him the whole truth. "Mr. Mahoney was busy and asked me to take Mr. Koenig his mail."

"That's beyond the call of duty," Pops snapped. "Don't do it again."

"There's no job description," I returned. "I don't see how I can refuse any reasonable request. He doesn't live alone, you know. He has a housekeeper." I hoped the image of chaperone would placate my father.

"Is it a nice house?" Faye asked.

"It's gorgeous," I informed her eagerly. "It's one of those big old Victorian places, packed with antiques. But it's in perfect shape. Not dark and gloomy at all. It's just like one of those remodeled houses in the Sunday *Times* magazine section."

"I'd love to see it," she said.

"Maybe I can arrange it. I'll ask him next time."

"Next time?" Pops exploded. "What do you mean, next time?"

"I may very well be asked to deliver the mail

again some day. Or something else. It seems he does most of his work from his study at home."

I had seated myself on the floor next to Pops' chair, and he took my hand. "Izzie," he said, "why? Why did he want you to come to work for him? He could get an inexperienced helper anywhere. I still think he wants something from you. If not, then why you? Why not some kid from Denford who could walk over?"

Why. That was one question I hadn't gotten around to asking Leo Koenig. I shook my head. "Pops, you know what he looks like. That makes it hard for him to meet people. Interviews must be difficult for him. You were there, and that made it easier. He just had to ask you. Actually, I think he's rather shy. He's careful about the circumstances under which he sees people."

"What about me?" Pops exploded. "Was he careful when he met me?"

I didn't answer. I had no explanation. The man who had confronted Pops in a demanding fury bore almost no resemblance to my dinner host, at least not in his behavior.

"Really, darling," Faye said, "I don't think there's anything to worry about. Izzie has worked there for almost two weeks and nothing has happened. She's never alone with him anyway."

Pops sighed, and it sounded like air escaping from a balloon.

I stood up and patted his head. "I may be sent to his house again, but I may not be. So don't worry about it."

I hadn't been invited again for a particular day. But I knew I would be. And I knew too that I would go. However horrifying Leo was to look at, he was fascinating to listen to. My life wasn't so interesting that I could afford to pass up the opportunity.

I continued never to see him at work, though I began, inevitably, to encounter some of the other employees. A half dozen or so men and women tended the greenhouses, and there were, in addition, a driver for the delivery truck and a sort of secretary-receptionist-bookkeeper who was holed up in a little office next to the workroom where Dilly and I spent our time. It was she I got to know first, after Dilly and Mr. Mahoney, if it could be said I really knew them. I didn't really know Agnes either, though we now spoke when we met. As a matter of fact, Dilly was the only deaf-mute working for Leo Koenig, but because of their lack of communicativeness, the rest may as well have been. It was as if they were all hiding some kind of secret and were afraid that if they spoke casually they might inadvertently let it out.

Saturday I found another dinner invitation in my pay envelope for the following Thursday night. I noticed that I was not docked for the hours I had spent at Leo's house. In his mind did they count as work?

The menu was different on the second occasion and so were the things we talked about, but the pattern of the evening was much the same as on the previous occasion. Mr. Mahoney was present the entire time, but never participated in the conversation. The cab appeared promptly at nine, and I was home before nine-thirty. When I first laid eyes on Leo, I shivered with a disgust I could not conceal. And yet, by the time the second visit was over, though I still avoided gazing at him directly, I realized I was perfectly relaxed in his company.

We looked at a magnificent volume of full-color prints of the works of Leonardo da Vinci, a topic we had come to through a complicated conversational route that had begun at the dinner table when I had asked him to tell me more about Italy, and that had evolved into a discussion of the entire Renaissance. Leo was pointing out the fact that the Mona Lisa, like him, lacked eyebrows when we heard the honk of the cab's horn.

He shut the book and pushed it toward me. "Take it," he said. "Look at it at your leisure."

"That isn't necessary," I said. "It's so heavy. I'll look at it some more next time I come."

"No," he urged. "Take it. I want you to have it."

"You mean to keep?"

"Yes," he said. "To keep."

"I couldn't," I protested.

"Why not? Don't you like it?"

"Well, sure, I like it," I returned. "What's not to like? But then, you like it too. And it's so expensive."

"It's only a book," he responded dryly. "Not a jewel. And I have plenty of other books about Leonardo." He gestured toward the shelves that almost buckled beneath the heavy burden of his enormous collection of art books. He didn't go to museums any longer, he had explained earlier, so he had acquired the handsomest books published to satisfy his appetite for art. "Please take it. I will be deeply offended," he added, "if you do not."

For the first time since I'd entered his study that evening, I felt a touch of discomfort. But I accepted the gift, feeling that it would be truly unkind to refuse it. I'd try to get it into my room before I saw Pops and Faye. If I didn't, and they noticed it, I'd say it came from the library. Mr. Mahoney carried it out to the cab.

Again, Leo walked me to the door. Again, when we reached it, he said, very quietly, "Isabel, will you kiss me good night?"

Even though I was totally incapable of a positive response, this request, unlike the gift of the book, curiously caused me no discomfort whatsoever, perhaps because I felt that he didn't really expect me to acquiesce. I merely said, as I had the week before, "I'm sorry, Leo, but I can't do that." I extended my hand, indicating my willingness to shake his. He looked down at his claw, and with a barely visible shake of his head, placed it around the doorknob and opened the door.

"You will come again, though, won't you?" he asked. The humility with which he issued that invitation wrenched my heart.

"Of course, if you want me to," I said.

"I do," he replied. "More than anything."

And again, when I ran down the porch steps, I turned to see him illuminated in the doorway. "Good night," he called.

I waved. "Good night, Leo. Sleep well."

The visits became a weekly habit. I knew he looked forward to them, because he told me so, point-blank. I looked forward to them too. He was the first adult I'd ever known who treated me absolutely as an equal. With him, I felt as if I were entirely grown-up.

That was partly because of his manner toward me, and partly because of the things we talked about. I asked him a lot of questions, because he knew so much, but he asked me a lot of questions too and seemed really to care about what I thought. Would I vote for President Reagan if he ran again? Did I support the nuclear freeze movement? If I had the power to change my high school, how would I use it? Did I believe in God? Did I think there was intelligent life on other planets?

He didn't ask those questions out of the blue. They grew from conversations we had about books or articles we had read or TV programs we had watched.

One thing simply led to another so that the three hours I was with him each Thursday night seemed scarcely more than three minutes—except for that one minute at the end when he asked me, always, if I would kiss him good night, and I answered, always, "No." That one minute was in itself an eternity.

We talked about personal things too. At least, I did. I told him about Pops and Faye and Mimi and her wedding. "I know Mimi loves Neil," I said, "but lately I think the wedding itself—you know, the clothes, and the flowers, and the invitations—has grown so large in her mind she's almost forgotten about him. Of course," I added, to be fair, "that may be because he was just transferred to Houston, and thinking about the wedding keeps her from missing him too much."

"Isabel, do *you* have a boyfriend?"

I was so startled by his question that, involuntarily, I covered my mouth with my hand. He'd never asked me anything like that before. Until now, what I'd told him about my private life I had always volunteered. "No," I said shortly.

"How come?" he asked. "You're very beautiful. In my life I think I've only known one other girl as attractive as you. What's more, you're lively, intelligent, and talented. If you don't have a boyfriend, that must be your choice. Why?"

I leaned forward. "I don't think that's any of your business," I replied in a low voice. I gestured briefly in

Mr. Mahoney's direction. He was in the room with us as always.

"Come on, Isabel," he chided gently. Mostly he expressed emotions with his voice and gestures. His face wasn't capable of much movement. "Mr. Mahoney ignores us, just as we ignore him." Maybe the last part of his statement was true, but I wasn't so sure about the first part.

"Look, Leo," I said, "I don't know why I don't have a boyfriend, but I don't. I don't want one, I guess. Having a boyfriend nowadays is pretty complicated. Maybe I misplaced my century. But that's the way it is."

"Perhaps you're too attached to your father."

"Please, Leo, spare me your two-bit Freudian analysis." I was beginning to get really angry. "How would you like it if I started in on you? Wouldn't a shrink just love to get inside your head. You'd be a regular annuity for him."

He leaned back in his chair and laughed. He couldn't smile, but he could laugh. "Touché," he said. "You win. I'll drop the subject."

"Good." I shut my mouth firmly and did not say another word.

"Isabel!" He leaned forward again. "You're furious with me, aren't you? I'm sorry. I didn't realize I was hitting such a sensitive spot. Please forgive me."

I remained silent.

"Isabel, please." There was a note of desperation in his voice. "Say that you forgive me."

I relented. "If you promise not to mention it again, I forgive you."

"I promise. Now you promise not to stop coming."

"Oh, Leo, Leo, I had no intention of not coming again." I found his insecurity concerning me almost touching. He certainly never displayed it in any other area. "When I was in third grade," I explained reassuringly, "if I had a quarrel with a friend, we'd scream at each other 'I never want to see you again' and run home. I trust I'm past that now. After all, even then we didn't mean it."

Not only the visits but also the gifts became a weekly habit. I got accustomed to the money pretty quickly too. Every Monday I banked a hundred and eighty dollars, retaining thirty for my own use. I told Pops I didn't need an allowance now that I was working, but neither he nor Faye had any idea of how much money I was accumulating. I didn't tell them about the presents either. I felt to the depths of my soul that they were gifts of pure friendship, but how would I ever convince Pops of that? So the volume of paintings by Leonardo, the miniature seascape in oils standing on a tiny easel, the tape of Irish folk songs, and the hand-painted Japanese fan were treasures that lay incongruously on the shelves in my room among the stuffed bears, trolls and dusty dolls collected in my childhood.

I felt as if I were leading two lives. On the one hand were the florist shop and Leo's palace. That was a world that seemed located in its own order of reality, unconnected to my other, everyday, normal, mundane existence of home and school. The two spheres continued whirling side by side, without touching, and when I was in one of them I rarely spoke of the other one, hardly even gave the other one a thought—except sometimes in my room when I riffled the pages of the Leonardo book, or stared at the tiny painting, or opened and shut the fan.

Marla still wasn't speaking to me. Sunny didn't have much to say to me either. I guess she felt she sort of had to choose between Marla and me. I couldn't blame her for picking Marla. I wasn't around much.

Some days I walked to math class with Corky Benedetti and Rob. One afternoon Corky said, "Sal and I are going bowling tomorrow night. Helena's coming with us."

Rob didn't say anything. So I said, "That's nice."

"Helena and Gerry Fitzgerald," Corky added.

"I know Gerry and Helena are seeing each other," Rob said quietly. "They're entitled."

"Sal didn't tell me until after she'd made the arrangements."

"It's OK, Corky," Rob assured him. "Really, it is. Don't worry about me. I have plenty to do tomorrow night."

"Like what?" It was only after I'd spoken that I realized what I had done. I could tell from the expression on Rob's face as he replied that he realized it too. "I'm going to a computer show at the Morristown Armory. You want to come?"

"Sure," I said.

"I didn't know you were interested in computers."

"I'm not. But maybe I ought to be."

"To the movies, no. To a computer show, yes. Izzie Courtney, you're crazy."

I shrugged. "Take it or leave it." I figured Marla might as well hang me for a sheep as a lamb.

Corky looked from one of us to the other, a light bulb flashing inside his head. "I think Sal's up ahead. I'll catch you guys later," he said as he hurried away from us. Sal was nowhere in sight.

Laughing, I turned to Rob. He was laughing too. "It'll be all over the school in five minutes," he said. "Izzie and Rob are a thing."

"Izzie and Rob are friends," I replied firmly.

"Yeah, I know," he sighed. "Don't worry. I'll go easy. I know how skittish you are. We'll play by your rules, entirely."

"Until you get tired of them."

"Oh well. We'll worry about that when it happens."

So I went with him to the computer show Friday night, and it was pretty interesting. Rob was inspecting all the home models carefully. His father had said he could have one for his birthday.

"That's a nice gift," I said. Even the cheap ones that could barely do more than play a few games were pretty expensive. "Will it be like one of those model train outfits fathers sometimes buy their little kindergarten sons? Will it really be more for your dad than for you?"

"Not at all. My father says he can remember when bookkeepers didn't even have adding machines. He says he was born much too soon to make it into the computer age."

"But my dad uses one," I said, "in his office. He's smart, but I don't think he's any smarter than yours." Both of Rob's parents were professors at Rutgers. His father taught philosophy and his mother taught art history.

"You have to remember," he said, "that my parents are a lot older than yours." I had met them a couple of times, after plays or basketball games, and I had known that. "They didn't have me until Mom was forty-five and Dad was nearly fifty."

By now we were back in Rob's van, rolling along the dark, empty highway, just the two of us, all alone in a moving island, the only inhabited bit of space as far as our eyes could see. It was a setting that inspired confidences.

"Your mother never had a child until she was forty-five?" I said. Just as I had known Rob's parents were older, I also knew he was an only child. "Isn't that kind of dangerous?"

"To tell you the truth, at the time I don't think she much cared whether she lived or died. She felt better after I came along." In the shadowed interior of the van, I couldn't see the expression on his face. "Anyway, that's what she told me. You see," he explained, "she had had another kid. A girl who was killed in an automobile accident about a year and a half before I was born. She was twenty at the time."

"My God!" I exclaimed. "How terrible."

"Well, not for me," he allowed with a kind of rueful little laugh. "I never even knew her. And if she hadn't died, I guess I would never have been born. I don't think my mother would have had another baby at her age with her career and everything. But of course it was terrible for my parents. When I started to drive, for a while there I thought Mom was going to have a nervous breakdown."

"But you drove anyway."

"Well, I had to, didn't I? You can't live where we live and not drive. I'm careful. They know that."

"They got over it then," I said softly. "Your sister's death, I mean."

"Well, they never forgot. They have pictures of

her all over their bedroom." He took a deep breath. "But they went on. They even got to be happy again, sometimes. I mean, like you. You got over your real mother's death, didn't you?"

"I was awfully young when she died. I hardly remember her." That wasn't something I admitted very often. Actually, I don't think I'd ever spoken about my mother with someone of my own age before. "I guess I got over her. I don't know."

"Well, it leaves a scar. It has to," Rob said quietly. "But you go on. You live."

At my house he accompanied me to the door, but he didn't make a single move. He didn't even touch me, just like he'd promised. I invited him in for a Coke or some tea, but he said no; the next day he had to be at work by eight, and he'd better get home before it got too late.

After that, we walked together to math class every day and sometimes to other classes too. Most Friday and Saturday nights we saw each other. Lots of times we didn't go anyplace, but just stayed home and watched a movie on the cable. His house wasn't connected. His parents weren't much more into television than they were into computers. They had one elderly set with a twelve-inch screen in the house in case they needed to watch an earthquake or assassination, but that was as far as they'd go. When I questioned him about that, he said they'd offered to tie into the cable if he wanted it, but he told them he didn't have time for it during the week, and on weekends it was more fun to watch it at some girl's house. Maybe he said that to make me jealous, but it didn't. I didn't expect to last a long time in Rob's life. I knew he always fooled around with someone in between his on-again, off-again relationship with Helena.

Sometimes Faye and Pops stayed home and watched TV too. Actually, Faye didn't watch much. She was mostly jumping up and down getting things for Rob to eat. "Your mother is really crazy about me, isn't she?" Rob said as I walked him to his van after an evening during which she'd plied him with popcorn, beer, sandwiches, ice cream, and home-baked pie.

"Yeah," I agreed. "She thinks you're great."

"I wish a little of her feelings would rub off on you," he complained.

"You're free to quit any time, Rob," I said. "I'd miss you. You're fun. But I'd certainly understand."

"Oh well," he returned, his usual cheerfulness reasserting itself, "not yet. Especially not now that your father is talking about buying a VCR. Then I can watch *Star Wars* every single Saturday night."

"Not with me you won't."

He reached out his hand, and then dropped it again to his side. "I'm leaving," he said, "before I do something that will really make you mad." After that he left so quickly I barely had time to say good night.

Back in the house, I went to the kitchen to help Faye clean up from the eating marathon. "He's a sweetheart," she said as she loaded plates into the machine.

I began wrapping leftover sandwiches in plastic wrap. "Yeah," I agreed. "He's nice."

"But you didn't even kiss him good night, did you?" Her voice was cool, and she didn't look up from the dishwasher.

"How do you know?" I retorted sharply.

"You came in too fast," she said.

"I'm not in love with him."

"You don't have to be in love with a guy to kiss him."

I turned around to face her. "Faye, what is it with you? Why are you so concerned about my love life? You ought to be glad I am like I am. You don't have to worry about my getting pregnant or something like other mothers do."

"You're not normal," she accused. Now she straightened and looked at me. "You're not in love with that Leo, are you?"

"Faye, are you crazy? You heard Pops describe him. No one could be in love with him."

"No one normal."

"Come on, Faye."

"Hey, you promised you'd ask if I could see his house. I want to see it. It sounds gorgeous. Maybe I'll get some ideas. Did you ask yet?"

I was glad she'd changed the subject. It meant she'd just sort of been teasing when she asked me if I was in love with Leo. "No, I haven't asked yet," I said. "But I will. Next time I see him, I'll ask. I don't see him very often."

But I knew I'd never ask. I didn't want her in Leo's house. She'd taken over Rob. Leo was mine, my private special thing.

Eight

RIGHT AFTER EASTER we had a warm spell. The weather was more like June than April. Mr. Mahoney, Leo, and I sat out after dinner on a screened-in porch off to the side of the house. Huge wooden pots full of azaleas bloomed in the corners, orange and pink blossoms contrasting with the rocking chairs, couch, and chaise made of white wicker like the furniture on the front porch. Hurricane lamps burning kerosene had been set out next to arrangements of tulips and daffodils on the tables. The electrical fixture in the ceiling remained unlit.

For once, Leo was as silent as Mr. Mahoney. Stuffed with chicken cacciatore and rum cake, I was content to rock myself gently into a half-doze while

I breathed in the odor of jasmine. Jasmine in New Jersey. It was just one of the exotica growing in Leo's garden, kept alive all winter with smudge pots and plastic wrapping.

Suddenly, Leo spoke. "Shall we walk in the yard?" he suggested.

"I'm so comfortable," I protested.

"You're falling asleep. I don't ply you with delicacies so that you can take a nap. I do it for the sake of your company."

I shook my head briskly. "OK. A walk."

"Mr. Mahoney, would you be so good as to turn on the lights?"

"Sure." Mr. Mahoney leaped to his feet. "I'll wait for you in the study."

"No, Mr. Mahoney," Leo said. "You'll join us for a stroll. It'll do you good. You ate too much too."

"Let Mr. Mahoney read if he wants to," I interjected. I knew it wasn't the *National Geographics* that drew him to the study. It was the classy Canadian whiskey. There was no bar on the porch, and though Mrs. Mangarelli had brought out coffee, Mr. Mahoney preferred to fix his own drinks than to ask for them. "Really, Leo," I added quietly, "we don't need a chaperone."

He hesitated for a moment.

"I won't tell my father," I continued, glancing at him obliquely.

He nodded slowly. "All right." Then he rose from his seat, and I rose from mine. Mr. Mahoney went inside, and a second later, the entire garden was illuminated with lights that seemed to be concealed among the bushes and trees. It was not as bright as day —far from it—but we would have no difficulty finding our way along the paths without stumbling.

Leo opened the screen door, and I followed him down the steps that led to the flagstone terrace. A path of white pebbles wound through the thick green shrubbery and carefully tended beds, which by day were bright with the blooms of spring. We walked along it silently, slowly. It was cooler than it had been just a few minutes before; a breeze had come up, and I shivered slightly.

Leo must have noticed. "The warmth of spring is treacherous," he said. "It never lasts through the night. Shall we go in?"

"I'm not really cold," I replied. "It's beautiful out here. Let's just walk a little faster."

He moved ahead of me quickly, and I stretched my legs with each step in an effort to keep up with his long stride. In a very few moments we had reached the hedges that formed the boundary between the back yard and the grounds surrounding the shop. "The property is deceiving," Leo said. "Because of the way we've laid out the gardens, we appear to be sitting in the middle of acres and acres. Actually, there are only two."

"How long have you lived here?" I asked.

"All my life," he replied. "I was born in this house. I intend to die in it."

"You'll die in a hospital like everyone else," I told him.

"No I won't," he insisted. "When I get sick with my fatal disease, I'm just going to die from it. I'm not going to let anyone do anything to save me."

I was deeply shocked. "That's a terrible thing to say. Why do you want to die? You have everything here."

"My God, Isabel," he exclaimed, "how can you say that? You see what I look like. If you had my face instead of yours, you'd just as soon be dead too."

For a moment, surrounded by perfect loveliness, I had actually forgotten his poor ravaged face! And yet, what I had said had not been wrong, not completely. "All right, so you feel sorry for yourself. I don't blame you. But it *is* wonderful here. You do have all of this, and the taste and the brains to appreciate it."

"And the money to have created it," he added. "It didn't look like this when I was growing up here, believe me. But all I've built is a prison—no doubt an exquisite prison, but a prison nonetheless."

"Because you choose it to be one."

He turned so that his eyes were looking directly into mine. It was a position he rarely assumed. Even though the glow from hidden lights was not bright enough to reveal his features in detail, I shuddered slightly. "Do you like me, Isabel?" he queried sharply.

"You know I do," I replied, forcing my face to remain turned toward his.

"And still you shudder when you see me. So does Mr. Mahoney. So does Dilly. So does Mrs. Mangarelli. So do they all. They like me too, and they're grateful to me. And still they shudder." He shook his head angrily. "I resent your accusation of self-pity. I regard self-pity as the least attractive of human emotions. My isolation is merely an entirely realistic response to the situation that I find myself in. Isabel, don't presume. You know nothing about it."

Now I was annoyed. "It's all right for you to ask me personal questions and make comments about my private life." I had not forgotten the evening when he'd asked me if I had a boyfriend. "But I'm not supposed to have the same privilege, is that it? Well, if that's your idea of friendship, it isn't mine!" It was amazing, the things that I could say to him.

"Listen to me," he shot back. "Listen carefully. I don't pity myself, because I deserve this face. Why do you think I didn't kill myself years ago? Because I have to live out this punishment. I deserve it."

The intensity of his fury awed me. Suddenly I felt very small and very foolish. But still I asked my question. "You deserve your face? Why?"

"Come," he said. "I'll show you."

Again I followed his long-legged stride. He hurried back along the path that we had already traversed, and then veered off onto another one that led to the far corner of the essentially rectangular property. We came upon a building of the same yellowish stone as the main house, but somewhat smaller. Its steeply pitched roof boasted a cupola, atop which sat a weather vane. "This was the stable once," Leo said. "Now it's a garage." He tugged at the latch until the great cross-hatched door swung open. He stepped inside the cavernous opening and reached for a switch on the adjacent wall. The interior was immediately flooded with brilliant, glaring light.

I blinked rapidly a few times as I entered, and sniffed the odor of gasoline, behind which I seemed to sense a lingering trace of the warm smell of hay and horse manure. The remodeled stable had room for four cars. In one bay rested the Mercedes in which Mr. Mahoney had picked me up the very first day I had come to work at Castle Florists. In the second bay was an old station wagon. The third contained a small shiny tractor, accompanied by an array of lawn-mowing, leaf-raking, and general gardening attachments.

But it was toward the fourth bay that Leo headed and I followed. It contained a blackened wreck. Parts had melted, and then hardened again in fantastic shapes bearing no resemblance to whatever they had been before. The front end was squashed like a folded accordion, and the innards dangled loosely in incomprehensible disarray. The steering wheel had pushed right through the back of the driver's bucket seat. The roof was full of deep dents and pits. The front wheels were gone; the back tires were in shreds. All the windows that could still be recognized as windows were empty of glass. The door on the passenger side had collapsed inward completely. The door from the driver's side leaned against the rear wall of the garage.

Leo spoke. "That was once a Maserati sports car. It was magnificent—very expensive and very fast. Even twenty-odd years ago, when I bought it, it cost eighteen thousand dollars. I could not at the time afford it, but I bought it anyway. My father had just died and left me some money. He'd been a successful lawyer, but, like me, a big spender. I didn't inherit as much as I'd expected, but I didn't let that stop me. My mother was long dead. I saw no reason not to do exactly what I wanted to do. Or thought I wanted."

He paused. I remained silent for a moment, and then I said softly, "Go on, please."

"Oh, I was the most arrogant young bull you've ever encountered. I was free of a father I'd never liked very much, and who certainly had never given much evidence of liking me. I was as handsome then as you're beautiful today. I had all the girl friends I could use—and I did use them, freely, and without giving them a moment's more thought than I gave a rose that I clipped from one of my bushes. I really must have believed that all people were on earth solely for what use I could make of them. Of course, no one loved me. But that was all right. I didn't love anyone either. Love, if I ever thought about it at all, seemed nothing but an encumbrance, an obstacle in the way of a good time."

He leaned against the collapsed front door of the ruined Maserati, and talked. I leaned on the garage wall and hugged myself against the chill of the stale, damp air, and listened.

"But after a couple of years, I did find myself spending more time with one particular girl than with any of the others. I even took her to Europe with me on a couple of trips. Her name was Martha. That's what she was always called, Martha. She didn't have any kind of a nickname, even though her own name sounded so prim and proper. It was totally at odds with her personality. She came from a brilliant family, and she was extraordinarily bright herself. She was their only child, and they'd spoiled her, I suppose. She wanted to be an actress, and she'd starred in all the high school plays." His eyes focused on me momentarily. "Like you. Now that I think about it, although she probably was quite talented, I don't think she really had the discipline to pursue such a difficult profession. Anyway, I didn't care about her career plans. What mattered to me at the time was that she was absolutely stunning, and that she liked a good time as much as I did. She told me that it was all that matters while you're young. She said there'd be time enough to be serious later. Though up until then, I'd preferred older women, I went out with her a lot. She was four years younger than I. If she were alive today, she'd be close to forty. She'd probably have calmed down by now. Most everyone does. She'd have married, had a couple of kids. Her parents would have grandchildren. . . ."

Again, silence descended between us. It didn't take any great intuitive leap to figure out what had happened. "I guess I know how she died," I said.

But saying that could not spare him the pain that reciting the story had to cause him. Like the Ancient Mariner's, his was a tale he was obliged to tell.

"She loved my car," he said, as if he hadn't even heard my comment. "I could never go fast enough to suit her. One night we had a big fight. We were always having furious arguments. It was part of the excitement between us. And we drank a lot, which made us quarrelsome. Even when we were smoking grass, we drank. Has anyone done a study, do you think, of what happens when you combine pot and alcohol?"

It was merely a rhetorical question. He did not pause in his recital. "We had the fight at a party. She wanted to go home; I didn't want to leave. I told her she could walk. But it was raining hard, and when she started for the door, I jumped up and went with her, figuring I'd drive her home and come back to finish what I'd started with a new girl I'd just met that night. It was she Martha and I were quarreling about. Martha said all she wanted was a good time, but if that was true, why was she so jealous? I was so furious with her, and she was so furious with me, that once we were on our way, we were still yelling at each other. My mind was anyplace but on the road. It was so dark and rainy, I scarcely knew where I was going. If I'd been even halfway sober, I'd have been scared out of my wits. She saw the headlights of the oncoming car first, and she panicked. I guess to her, in the rain and the dark, it looked as if it was in our lane. She screamed and grabbed my arm. I lost control, and we skidded on the wet road and hit the car coming in the other direction. I have absolutely no memory of what happened after that. I was out for days. When I woke up in the hospital, my face and hands were covered with bandages, and they told me Martha was dead. The engine had exploded. I didn't know it, but I had stumbled out of the car a second before that happened, and, thank God, so had the driver of the other car. He had been alone. They couldn't get Martha's body out of the seat until after they'd put out the fire. They found me on the ground on the passenger side. They think I was burned trying to get the door open. They told me they were sure she had died instantly, at the moment of impact. I hope they were telling me the truth."

He stopped talking, put his head down, and covered his face with his hands. "Couldn't they have done plastic surgery?" I asked. My words sounded absurdly banal in my own ears.

"On me?"

"Yes."

His hands fell to his sides, but he turned his head so that I could not see his face. "I'd still be undergoing operations if I'd let them get started with that," he said. "There was no guarantee anyway that they'd have done much good. I did let them reconstruct my hands. I had to be able to work. I'd always gardened as a hobby, though I didn't start the business until after I got out of the hospital." He flexed his clawlike fingers. "They're not very pretty," he said, "but they're entirely serviceable."

He kept his face, as he kept the wreck of the car, to remind him always of his guilt. I hesitated, but then I spoke. So what if he got mad at me? "Listen, Leo," I said, "you'll have every right to be as angry with me as I was with you a few weeks ago, but I'm going to say this anyway. Did you ever—well, did you ever think of getting some help?"

"You mean a shrink?" Not anger, but derision infused his tone. "They wanted me to, in the hospital. I was in that place for nearly six months. I was at their mercy. They sent one in, but I wouldn't talk to him, and they couldn't make me. What did I need a shrink for? To tell me I had no reason to feel guilty?

I had a very good reason to feel guilty, the best in the world. I may not be worth much, Isabel, but if I didn't feel guilt over what I'd done, I'd be worth less than nothing. Guilt is the only thing that makes me human."

"What about your intelligence?" I countered. "Your sense of humor? Your compassion? Your talent? They don't count?"

His head shot up, and once again, I was confronted by his ruined face. "No wonder I like you, Isabel. When I'm with you, I can almost imagine I'm not a monster."

We went back to the house. It was already a quarter after nine. Not knowing how long we'd be gone, Mr. Mahoney had sent the cab away when it had come. He'd drive me home himself, he said.

That night Leo didn't give me any sort of a gift. But he asked me the same question he always asked me. "Isabel, will you kiss me good night?"

I lifted my eyes to his face. Almost, almost I was tempted to acquiesce, so filled was I with pity for him. But even I knew pity was not reason enough. "No, Leo," I replied, as I always replied. "I'm sorry, but I can't let you do that." And then I ran out the door, down the steps, and out to the car with all the speed I could muster.

I didn't care how much Mr. Mahoney disliked questions. I was resolved to ask him some that night, and persist until I got answers. "Mr. Mahoney," I said as soon as I was settled next to him in the front seat of the Mercedes, "how long have you worked for Leo?"

"Eighteen years," he replied shortly.

"Then you came to work for him right after he got out of the hospital."

He shot me a sidelong glance. "I met him in the hospital," he said. Then, surprisingly, he continued. "I had just gotten out of jail. I'd been in for seven years for armed robbery. I'd held up a gas station, shot and wounded a guy. It wasn't the first time. I'd been in and out of jail from the time I was sixteen. This last time I was out less than a month when my appendix burst, and I landed in the hospital almost dead. They put me in the same room with Leo. I guess they figured I was tough enough to handle what he looked like. At first he was really mad. He wanted a private room. They forced me on him—thought a roommate would do him good, I guess."

"I guess they were right," I said.

"For him, I don't know. For me it was one hell of a lucky break. When I didn't throw up at the sight of him, he decided it was OK to talk to me. What he did mostly was ask questions. He got my whole life story out of me. No one else has ever done that. He found out I'd worked on the prison farm. I'd kind of liked that. He'd run through a lot of money by then, and was planning to open up a florist business with what was left, so he offered me a job. First time in my life I'd been offered a legitimate job, no strings attached." Mr. Mahoney's laugh was thin and dry, scarcely a laugh at all. "I've been straight ever since. Pays me so well there's no point to stealing. I'd had enough of that life anyway. I'd had enough of it for a long time before. But other times, I went back. Couldn't get a legit job. The only ones who wanted me were guys I'd known from before."

"Dilly said something similar," I said. "She said no one else would hire her."

"He pays Dilly good too," Mr. Mahoney said.

I was glad to find out I wasn't the only one.

"He pays us all good. And we're all freaks, in one way or another. Like him. Freaks. Except you, of course."

I wasn't so sure of that, but I let it pass. "Mrs. Mangarelli?" I queried.

"Mrs. Mangarelli's husband beat her. One day she just took his hunting rifle and shot him. She served time."

"Agnes?"

"She's got two retarded kids. They're in the state home and she goes to see them every Sunday. One's so bad he don't even know who she is. And the others, who work in the greenhouses, every one of them has a story they'd just as soon not tell you."

"They sure are a silent bunch," I agreed. I wanted to ask him what had made him so suddenly communicative. I had resolved to get some answers out of him, no matter how much effort it took, but it had taken almost no effort at all.

As if in reply to the words I hadn't spoken, Mr. Mahoney said, "You found out something tonight. Probably a lot. Could tell just by looking at your face. Figured no harm in your finding out more. He'd never have told you if he thought you were a blabbermouth."

"What happened to him is no secret," I said. "It must have been in all the papers. Everyone in Denford must know about it."

"It was a long time ago, and the girl's family moved right after the accident. People around here don't think about it anymore. The town takes him as he is. They never see him. They just know he's rich, and they write to him for contributions to the United Way and the Rescue Squad and the Boy Scouts and all the rest of it. He gives too, plenty. Agnes simply writes the checks. You can be sure he don't go to no Chamber of Commerce meetings. He don't want to be seen, and he don't want to be talked about."

"Which is fine with me," I said. "I have no one to talk about him to."

An untruth, as it turned out. But I could not have known that when I said it.

Inside, a reception committee awaited me. It consisted of only one person, Faye. Pops was out of town; he'd gone to a commodity brokers' convention in Chicago.

She was sitting in the living room. Since she never went in there except to clean or entertain company, it was clear that she intended to make sure she saw me the minute I walked through the front door. "Izzie," she said. "Come here, please. I want to talk to you." She laid the magazine she'd been pretending to read on the sofa beside her.

I stood in the archway between the front hall and the living room. "Shoot," I said.

"You'd better come in and sit down."

"Gee, Faye," I said, "I still have homework. It's getting late." The night's revelations had done me in. I didn't feel like talking anymore.

"You're supposed to be home by nine-thirty. What kept you?" I started to reply, but she interrupted me. "Please, Izzie, sit down."

"Mr. Mahoney drove me home," I said. "The cab never came." That was, of course, a fib, but certainly the least of the lies I'd told Faye and Pops since I'd started dining with Leo Thursday nights.

I entered the room and took a chair opposite the sofa on which she was sitting. "Izzie, I want you to tell me what's going on," she said, her hands folded on her lap, her eyes looking directly into mine.

"Faye, I don't know what you mean."

She reached into the pocket of her Sergio Valente jeans and pulled out a bank book. She held it up. "This is yours," she said.

"I can see that," I answered coldly. "What are you doing with it?"

"I found it in your room. I went in there to put your clean laundry on your bed, and I saw it lying on your table."

"And so you picked it up and looked in it? What made you think you had the right to do that?" As a rule I made my weekly deposit Monday at lunchtime, but I had been helping with the drama club pretzel sale during lunch the first three days of the week and hadn't gotten to the bank until earlier that Thursday. And then, as always, in a hurry when I'd arrived home after school, I'd left the bank book on my bed table instead of taking the time to put it away in my jewelry box where I usually kept it.

"I wanted to see if you were saving any of your money."

A very lame excuse, I thought. "Why didn't you just ask me?"

"Pardon me." Her tone was as chilly as mine. "I had no idea a bank book left out on a table was such a private thing."

"Would you show me yours?" I queried sharply.

"Anytime," she replied loftily.

But I didn't believe her. And I was very angry.

"I regard this as an inexcusable invasion of my privacy," I said.

"Well, that's not the issue I want to talk about."

"It's the one I want to talk about. I don't ever want you to look into anything that belongs to me again without my express permission. You don't even have to go into my room. Just leave the laundry on the machine and I'll take it up. As a matter of fact," I added quickly, "why should you do my laundry at all. I'm not seven years old any longer. I ought to be doing it myself."

"OK," she said. "You're right."

"I am?" The suddenness of her capitulation certainly took the wind out of my sails.

"Yes. I won't go into your room without an invitation, and I won't do your laundry."

"Well, that's good," I remarked, somewhat inadequately, as I stood up.

"But that's not what I want to talk about. You said your piece. Now let me say mine."

So I sat down again.

"It isn't only the bank book," she said. She was pushing at the cuticles of her nails the way she did when she was a little nervous. "I noticed some other things in your room. A fan, a little painting, some art books. Rob didn't give you those."

"Of course not. Why would Rob give them to me?"

"Precisely. Why would anyone give them to you? They're from *him,* aren't they? Your boss."

I shrugged. "Sure. So what?" But I felt much more uncomfortable than I let her know.

"And he pays you an absurd salary for a seventeen-year-old with no experience. Your bank book told me that. You led us to believe you were making minimum wage like all the other kids."

"I never said that."

"It's what we thought."

"I can't help what you thought."

"I imagine you've been delivering the mail to his house rather often lately."

Her tone implied no judgment, but I sensed the accusation behind her words. "What do you mean by that?" I snapped.

She stood up and walked toward me. "Izzie, please," she said quietly, "don't shut yourself away from me. Please. I want to help you. You know how upset your father's going to be. He hasn't trusted your Mr. Koenig since he first laid eyes on him." She sat down in the chair next to mine. "Izzie, he's got to be up to something. I don't want you going there anymore. I think it would be best if you'd quit the job. Your dad and I will help you to find another one." She patted my hand. "If things go as well for your father during the last part of the year as they have in the first, you won't need to work. He'll be able to pay for your European trip himself."

I pulled my hand away from hers and shoved it in my pocket. "I like my job. I like working. I like making my own money."

"In this world, Izzie, there's nothing for nothing," she said sharply. "You're old enough to realize that."

"Mr. Koenig is my friend," I said. "That's all he wants from me. Friendship. I won't stop going there. That would kill him altogether. He doesn't deserve that."

"Kill him? That's rather an extreme statement, Izzie. Let him find some friends his own age."

"He's not so old," I protested. "He's in his early forties, that's all."

"Izzie, I'm thirty-seven. I'm sure you don't think of me as so young!"

She was right. I didn't. To tell the truth, I didn't think of Leo as young either. To me he seemed as old as his house, maybe older. I decided to change my tactics. I took my hand out of my pocket and seized hers. "Faye, I appreciate your concern. Really, I do. But Mr. Koenig means me no harm. I know that. I won't take any more gifts from him, if that's what's troubling you, but I won't stop working for him or talking to him when he wants to talk." Perhaps she would have been convinced of Leo's goodwill if I told her the story he had told me that evening, the story I had assured Mr. Mahoney I'd have no occasion to repeat. And I still had no intention of repeating it.

Anyway, her suspicions aroused, the story would probably have had precisely the opposite effect from the one I desired.

"Well," Faye said, "we'll talk about it some more when your father gets home."

"There's nothing to talk about."

"We'll see." She stood up once again. "I feel like a cup of tea. You want one?"

For now, the subject was closed. I was certainly not going to be the one to reopen it. "No, thanks," I said. "I've got work to do. Good night, Faye."

I left her and ran up the stairs, two at a time. Once inside my own room, I shut the door and locked it. I'd never, ever done that before.

Nine

POPS CAME HOME FROM CHICAGO late Saturday night. Sunday morning we went through the whole business all over again, only it was worse. Of course it had to be worse. When I was being honest with myself, I knew I didn't give a damn for Faye's opinion of whatever I was or was not doing. I did for my father's.

"I don't want you going to that man's house ever again," Pops said. "And I want you to quit working for him." Faye nodded approvingly.

"But, Pops," I protested, "I need the money."

"You do not need the money," he exclaimed. "I will see to it that you go to Europe, if that's what you want to do. When have you ever been denied anything that you wanted?"

"Oh, Pops," I cried, "that's not the point."

"Izzie, that man is dangerous. I said so from the beginning. It was a mistake to allow you to go there in the first place. I can't imagine what got into me."

"Faye thought it was a fine idea."

"It's not your mother's fault. I have no one to blame but myself. Well, a mistake is no sin. The sin is in not trying to rectify it."

"You have the wrong impression of Leo, Pops, really you do. If you could meet him now, you would see that—"

"Leo, is it? Leo? You call your boss Leo?"

"Oh, Pops," I sighed. "This is getting impossible. Everyone calls him Leo."

No matter what I said, he was taking it the wrong way.

"Yes," he agreed, "it *is* getting impossible. That's why I absolutely insist you not see him anymore. You have to stop going to his house, and you have to stop working for him."

"You're ordering me?" I cried. "Ordering me? What is this, the nineteenth century? I'm your chattel, your possession?"

He didn't explode with anger. His voice was controlled and quiet as he answered me. "As long as you live under my roof, you must do as I say. You know my only concern is your safety. I don't deserve to be spoken to in the tone of voice you have just used, but I'll forget about that. You're under a strain. But just remember, when you're through with school, working at a job that pays a salary you can live on, supporting your own apartment, you can see whomever you please. Until then, I have to trust my own judgment on matters like this, and you have to trust it too. You don't have any choice." He'd never spoken to me like that before.

"Pops, I have to give notice." I was clutching at straws. "I can't just not show up."

"You can phone. I can't believe you're so skilled at your work that they will find you irreplaceable."

"Pops, Mr. Koenig deserves more than a phone call. I have to tell him in person. I don't want him to think I'm mad at him or anything. He's always been perfectly considerate and kind."

"Why should he care how you feel about him? Just phone him."

"He does care. He does care. I told you. The only thing he ever wanted from me was friendship."

"Friendship," Faye spat out. "Oh, Izzie, at your age, such naïveté is appalling."

"Not appalling," Pops said. "Attractive."

"I am *not* naïve," I cried. "I am not. All I'm saying is that you don't understand him. You don't understand what he wants."

"He never made a pass?" Faye queried. "He never made a move in your direction?"

"No," I said. And I blushed. For of course he had. Every time. "Isabel, will you kiss me good night?" But to call that formally phrased request a "pass," a "move," was to twist its meaning deliberately. It seemed to me that Pops and Faye were the naïve ones. Pops apparently had only one way of interpreting any generous action between a man and a woman. And that he could imagine Leo Koenig forcing himself upon another human being was merely evidence of his complete misunderstanding of Leo Koenig's character. "I was never alone with him anyway," I added. That was nearly true. How careful he had been to ensure no misinterpretation of our encounters—all, apparently, to no avail.

"That was merely to lull you into a false feeling of security," Faye said. "Sooner or later he would have told his lackey to disappear."

The three of us had been sitting at the kitchen table, but now I stood up. "I don't have to listen to this," I said. "I'm getting out of here."

"Young lady, where do you think you're going?" That was Faye.

"For a walk," I said. "Or maybe a ride. Yes, a ride. I'll call Rob and ask him to take me for a ride."

Perhaps they suspected what I was up to. And perhaps they decided to pretend they didn't, since I was doing it with Rob and was therefore presumably safe. In another two weeks, I wouldn't need Rob. I'd have my license and could drive myself where I needed to go. On the other hand, it would have been difficult to borrow Faye's or Pops' car for this particular errand.

Then again, maybe they had no suspicions whatsoever.

In the hall I picked up the phone and dialed Rob. "Rob," I said, "I need a ride. Could you help me out?"

"Sure," he said. "I'll be right over."

"You don't have to come in," I said. "I'll be waiting outside."

I ran upstairs and dressed quickly. Then I went outside to wait for Rob. Pops and Faye must have heard me leave, but they didn't say anything. I didn't have to wait long. Rob's van pulled up to the curb and I jumped up from the bottom step on which I'd been sitting and ran to meet him.

"What's up, doc?" he called through the open window.

I didn't answer until I had climbed in beside him. "I have to go to Denford," I said. "I have to tell my boss I can't work for him anymore."

Rob put his foot on the gas, and we moved out into the street. "I thought it was such a great job. I thought you loved it."

"Pops and Faye say I have to quit."

"Why?"

"They're afraid of him—afraid he might hurt me."

"What?"

"If you saw him, it'd shake you up too. He really looks like something out of a monster movie." I didn't go into detail.

"I don't know," Rob mused with a shake of his head. "From what I've seen of your folks, it just doesn't seem like them to be prejudiced that way. To judge a guy by his appearance, I mean."

"I guess they feel if you look like that it can affect your character," I tried to explain. "It's because it's me, you know. If I'm not involved, Pops can be perfectly objective about any man." I touched his arm briefly. "Thanks for the lift. I felt that someone who'd been so nice to me was entitled to more than a phone call. Pops and Faye disagreed, so I also felt I couldn't ask one of them to drive me over."

Suddenly Rob grinned. "Hey," he said, 'it's not so bad. Now you'll have more time for me!"

Miserable as I was, I couldn't help grinning too. "Rob, you have the patience of Job."

"Izzie, you're not really made of ice. You can't hold out on me forever."

"Can't I, now? You'll see."

But I couldn't sustain a jocular exchange. Rob realized that, and left me alone. We drove the rest of the way in silence.

Once we got to Denford, I directed Rob to the house. "Shall I come in with you?" he asked.

"I'd rather you didn't," I said.

"I'll wait here then."

"Oh, don't,' I urged. "Go back to the highway, get something to eat at Dunkin Donuts. I'll meet you right out here in half an hour."

He nodded his agreement. I opened the door and hoped out of the van. "Maybe I should wait until I'm sure you're inside," he said. "Maybe he won't be home."

"He'll be home. He never goes anywhere." The entry to the house was entirely invisible from the street. If Rob waited, I'd have had to come all the way back to tell him he could leave. He didn't move the van for a long as I could see him. By the time I reached the front porch, I couldn't tell if he was gone or not.

There was no bell. I lifted the heavy door knocker and let it fall back against the brass plate. I waited a few moments, and then I did it again. And again. But I didn't grow impatient. I knew it would be a long time before anyone opened the door in this house to which uninvited visitors never came.

After I'd knocked a fourth time, a woman's voice called, "Who's there?" It was Mrs. Mangarelli.

"Me, Isabel," I replied.

Slowly, disbelievingly, the door swung open. "Isabel," Mrs. Mangarelli said, as if to affirm the evidence of her eyes. "What do you want? It isn't Thursday."

"That's right, Mrs. Mangarelli. It's Sunday. But I have to see Leo anyway. Will you please tell him I'm here?"

"He doesn't see anyone—"

"Mrs. Mangarelli, he sees me. You *know* he sees me."

"Come in, Isabel." Leo had materialized suddenly in the hall behind her. He must have been listening from the front parlor. "It's all right, Mrs. Mangarelli. I'll take care of Isabel."

She shrugged and stepped aside as I entered the hall. "Come, Isabel," Leo said. "We'll talk in the study." I followed him down the hall, while Mrs. Mangarelli shut the front door and then disappeared into the kitchen.

We took our accustomed seats. It was warm; no fire burned in the grate. But still he kept his face turned toward the mantel, as usual, so I could see only his profile. "Would you like some coffee?" he asked.

"I had breakfast," I replied. Actually, I had eaten nothing. I lapsed into silence.

For a few moments he didn't say anything either. When he finally spoke, his deep voice was gentle and quiet. "You know I'm always pleased to see you, Isabel. But I don't think you simply dropped by to say hello. Will you tell me why you came?"

"I came to say good-bye." The words sounded so

bald, so final. But I didn't know how to put a better face on them.

His body stiffened, and instinctively he turned his face toward mine. Then, remembering, he turned away again. "Good-bye? What do you mean?"

"My father says I can't work for you anymore. He never wanted me to, really. Now Faye agrees with him. She used to be on my side—at least so far as you were concerned. But she isn't any longer, and so there's no one to talk him out of it."

"What about you, Isabel?" he asked. "Do you want to work for me?"

"Of course I do. I want to work for you, and visit you, and be your friend."

"Well, then—"

"Oh, Leo, Leo." I stood up and walked over to him. Then I knelt in front of him. I took his poor claws in my two hands and looked up into his terrible face. "He's my father. I live in his house. He doesn't make many rules for me. But on this he absolutely insists. I can't do anything about it, other than move out. I'm not prepared to go that far."

With a kind of deep shudder that shook his whole body, he pulled his hands away from mine. "I will never see you again. Never."

"Leo, of course you will," I said, rising to my feet. "Don't be so melodramatic. He'll come around eventually. Just give me some time to work on him."

"Then why did you say you'd come to say good-bye?"

"Well, I am saying good-bye—for now."

"Isabel, this will kill me. You're my friend. My only friend."

"Mr. Mahoney's your friend. Mrs. Mangarelli's your friend. Dilly's your friend. Agnes is your friend. They're all your friends."

"They're people who are grateful to me. You're my friend. You don't owe me anything. You came to me of your own free will."

"You gave me a job. You gave me presents."

"Isabel, if I hadn't, would you have behaved any differently toward me?"

Mutely, I shook my head. I wasn't at all sure if my denial held true for the beginning of our relationship, but it was certainly true now.

He said it again. "You're my friend. My only friend."

I felt a wave wash over me, a wave of anger. "You put too great a burden on me," I cried. "I'm not responsible for you! Don't blame me for your misery. Go out and do something about it yourself."

"Isabel! I explained—"

"You explained all right. But an explanation isn't necessarily an excuse."

"Isabel, I love you. . . ."

"Leo, I'm very fond of you. And I *will* see you

again. Don't make this any harder than it has to be."

"I don't believe it. I don't believe that you'll come back." His hand shaded his eyes; his voice sounded infinitely resigned, infinitely sad.

"I promise."

"You will forget me."

"How could I?"

He rose from his chair and looked me full in the face. I did not shiver; I did not tremble. He opened a small carved teakwood box that rested on the mantel. From it he took a little gold ring. Instead of a gem, it was set with a tiny carved cameo rose. He took my hand in his, and then he placed the little ring on my pinkie. "When you look at this," he said, "perhaps you will remember."

I didn't want to take another gift from him, but at that particular moment, how could I refuse? Although his face was not capable of much expression, his body, his voice, the black coals that were his eyes, all conveyed a misery so deep as to be beyond the power of words to define. "Thank you, Leo," I said. "I'll remember. I'll remember every moment of every day."

He laughed ironically. "Now you're the one who's being ridiculous, Isabel. I think you should go now. You can let yourself out. There is no point in prolonging this." He sat down again in his wing chair.

"All right." Good-bye had been a mistake. I tried a new phrase. "So long."

"Good-bye, Isabel."

I walked out of the room, down the hall, and out the front door. Then I started to run. I ran all the way down the front walk and out onto the sidewalk in front of the hedges that surrounded the house. The van was there. Rob had waited after all.

It was only afterward, when we were driving on the highway back to Winter Hill, that I realized something. Leo had never asked me why my folks had said I could not come to him anymore. It was as if he had known why without asking.

Ten

FOR A WHILE, Rob and I drove in silence. I was crying, and he let me cry. When we reached the A&P, he turned into the parking lot and pulled into a space along the side of the building.

I sniffled two or three times, wiped my eyes, and blew my nose with a crumpled Kleenex I had discovered in the pocket of my jeans. "Why are we stopping here?" I asked. "Do you have to pick something up for your mother?"

"No," he said quietly, "I don't have to go home. I thought I'd run in and buy some bread and cheese and fruit, and drive out to the reservoir. You want to come?"

"I won't be very good company," I said. "I don't feel much like talking."

"That's all right. I'll take you as you are."

"Sniffles and all?"

He nodded slowly, unsmilingly.

"OK."

He unlatched the van door. "'I'll only be a few minutes. While I'm inside, I'll call my folks so they'll know not to expect me for dinner."

"Do you think you could call my parents too?" I requested. "Or get your mother to call? I'm not ready to speak to them just yet."

He nodded again, hopped out of the van, slammed the door shut, and hurried into the market. By the time he came out again, I had managed to stop crying.

He dropped the paper bag full of groceries in the back, and then climbed in alongside of me once again. "I got potato chips and chocolate chip cookies and beer and Coke and tomatoes," he said. "Besides the bread and cheese and fruit."

"Just for the two of us?" I couldn't keep from smiling. "You must think I have the appetite of an elephant."

"Don't you get hungry when you're upset? I do."

"I usually have the opposite reaction," I explained. "I usually can't eat at all."

"Why didn't you tell me that *before* I went shopping?" he replied, grinning. Then his grin disappeared, and for the next few minutes, as he started up the motor and then negotiated the van out of the lot and back onto the highway, he said nothing.

I appreciated his sensitivity in leaving me alone, and I fell for a while into my own reverie. When he spoke again, although I realized he'd said something, I didn't quite catch his words. "What's that?" I queried, turning my head.

"He was more than just your boss, wasn't he?" Rob repeated.

"Yes. He's my friend. Faye and Pops can't prevent that."

"I'd like to meet him."

Faye had wanted to see his house. Now Rob wanted to see *him*. "I told you, that's impossible. He sees no one, except a few of his employees."

"And you, now that you're no longer one of them? Will he still see you?"

"Yes. I'll visit him again as soon as I can, as soon as it's possible."

"If you don't forget him."

"I won't forget him. What makes you think I could possibly forget him?"

Briefly, Rob glanced in my direction, his expression unreadable. Then he turned his eyes back to the road.

And, to tell the truth, I thought surprisingly little about Leo Koenig the rest of that day. The sun was brilliant, warm but not hot, and the air was sweet with the delicate odors and soft winds of spring. Rob got an old quilt from the back of the van and spread it out under a tree close enough to the reservoir to see the water, but far enough away so that we could barely hear the shouts of the children playing near their parents, whose blankets and picnicking equipment outlined temporary households scattered along the shore. The supplies Rob had stashed in the back of his van seemed unlimited: a tape player appeared, the Sunday paper, and pencils so we could do the puzzle. We ate and drank, we quarreled over who got to read the comics first, we walked in the woods, and when we came back, we pulled the quilt out into the sun and dozed for a while, lying side by side.

But my sleep was fitful and full of dreams peopled by dim figures I struggled to identify. When, despairing of any sort of meaningful rest, I struggled up into wakefulness and opened my eyes, I saw a black-browed boy of no more than four staring down at me. As soon as he decided I was sufficiently alert, he attacked me. "Is that your daddy?" he asked.

I glanced over at Rob. His eyes were shut, but the corners of his mouth twitched a little. I knew he was awake, and listening.

"No, he's not my daddy. He's too young to be my daddy."

"I mean your husband. Is he your husband?"

"No, he's not my husband."

The black-browed child wrinkled his nose and pursed his lips. "Is he your boyfriend?"

"He's my friend. And he's a boy."

"Then he's your boyfriend."

"That depends on what you mean by boyfriend."

Rob sat straight up; his eyes were now fully opened and bright with mischief. "Listen, kid, I'd like to be her boyfriend, whatever it means. You think you could talk her into it?"

The little boy stared at Rob, wide-eyed. Then he turned and made his way back down the bank toward the beach, his fat legs tumbling over each other in his haste. "You scared him," I said.

"More to the point, did I scare *you?*" Rob asked.

"You're my friend, Rob. Isn't that enough?"

"Your boss—your ex-boss—is your friend too. Everyone's your friend."

"You know that isn't true."

He let out a huge sigh and lay back again on the blanket. "Yeah, I know. I know it better than anyone."

"I have two friends. You and him. Right now, that's all."

He shut his eyes, as if he were trying to fall asleep again.

"Listen, Rob, my sister says I need a date for her wedding. You want to come?"

He bolted up immediately. "I'll come. I'd love to come."

"I wasn't sure. You don't like family occasions." I was remembering the immediate, if not the ultimate cause, of his breakup with Helena.

"A wedding is not a wake." He remembered too. "Besides, almost any occasion can be a good occasion if you're with the right person."

"I guess so. But don't get any ideas," I added hastily.

"What kind of ideas?"

"I'm just asking you to the wedding because I need a date. That's all."

"Geez, Izzie, you sure know how to hurt a guy." But his smile was jaunty as he spoke, and he patted my hand in a fatherly fashion.

Later, after he'd brought me home again, I put the cameo ring Leo had given me in the jewelry box on top of my bureau. The next morning, before I went to school, I removed it from the box and put it on my finger. After that, I wore it all the time, except when I was bathing or sleeping.

The wedding was almost upon us, and willy-nilly, I was swept up in the excitement. There was a lot to do, and Mimi wasn't home to do any of it. My particular job turned out to be travel plans. I spent hours after school on the phone with airlines and motels, trying to arrange the arriving flights of Pops' and

Faye's far-flung relatives and friends so as to hold to a minimum the number of trips I, with my brand-new driver's license, would have to make to the airport. I had to worry about all of Neil's relatives and friends too. He was not from Winter Hill but had met Mimi when she had worked in New York the previous summer, so every single one of the guests on his side was from far away. His parents were giving a dinner for the out-of-town company and the wedding party on Saturday night, but because they lived in Massachusetts, some of those arrangements fell on me too.

Although the cameo ring remained on my finger, after a few days my mind was so full of school and the wedding that there wasn't any room in it for anything else. I no longer thought of Leo every time I looked at it. Like my watch, and my mother's—my real mother's—locket, it had become just a piece of jewelry I always wore.

I saw a lot of Rob. He volunteered not only his van, but his own services as a chauffeur any time they were required. Faye and Pops were suitably grateful and assured him that they would keep his tank full of gas. They didn't wait until the actual weekend of the wedding to take him up on his offer, but decided that he and I should take an afternoon off from school and drive down to Philadelphia to pick up Mimi and all the goods she had accumulated in her student apartment during the two years she'd spent getting her M.B.A. Neil, who'd been transferred to Houston in February, wouldn't be arriving until two days before the wedding.

We drove south and west, keeping, at the beginning, to older roads that passed through rolling countryside dotted with towns and farms, instead of traveling the newer superhighways. We were in no hurry, and it was a glorious day at the end of May, perfect for a ride. "One of the ten best," Rob said.

"One of the ten best what?"

"Days," he said. "I make a list each year."

"How many have we had so far this year?"

He grinned. "This is the first."

"You have very high standards."

"New Jersey has very low weather. Well, there was that Sunday afternoon we spent at the reservoir," he admitted. "That was a beautiful day. But you were unhappy."

"You mean the people you know have to be in good spirits too if the day is to make your list? It's a wonder you come up with one a year, let alone ten."

"Not *all* the people I know." His hands tightened around the wheel, but his voice was light. "You're happier now, aren't you? You don't think about your old job so much anymore, do you?"

I felt a spasm of guilt twist my heart as I glanced down at the cameo rose on my finger. Until Rob had mentioned him, I hadn't given Leo a thought in three days, at least. Things I had learned from him were now a permanent part of my consciousness, but his image was growing dimmer and dimmer in my mind.

"I think of him," I said defensively. "Tonight when I get home, I'll try calling him again." But I wasn't at all sure that I would. In the beginning I had called, several times, both the house and the shop. It didn't matter whether Mrs. Mangarelli answered the phone, or Agnes, or Mr. Mahoney. They all told me Leo was out of town. I knew perfectly well that he never went anywhere. He was deliberately refusing to speak to me. I could understand that. Still, after half a dozen such rebuffs, I stopped calling.

In Philadelphia, we consumed a snack of limp celery, stale bagels, and elderly salami, the last of Mimi's leftovers, and then worked like galley slaves for the next couple of hours loading the van. Mimi had always been clever at avoiding any activity likely to generate perspiration, but this time she struggled up and down the stairs beneath huge cartons of pots and books as valiantly as Rob or I. Perhaps two years in her own apartment had changed her, or perhaps she was shamed by the example of Rob, a stranger, after all, who could not have worked any harder if she had been paying him movers' rates, which run to something like fifteen dollars an hour.

Late in the afternoon, she and I crouched on the

landing, struggling to retie a carton that had come undone. Blessedly, it was the last of a pile that had not so long ago loomed as high as Everest. Rob was down in the van, making room for it.

"He's crazy about you, isn't he? Are you crazy about him?" Mimi remarked conversationally as she tried yet again to force a recalcitrant pillow down under the flap of the box.

"Crazy about me? Rob? . . . Why don't you try sitting on the box while I tie it?"

"It's only made out of cardboard. It'll break. . . . Of course Rob. Who else is killing himself on behalf of your sister? He can't be doing it out of love for me."

"We're good friends, that's all," I insisted as I pulled the pillow out of the box. "We'll just have to throw this in on top of all the other stuff."

Now that the pillow had been removed, Mimi was able to refasten the string. She pulled the knot tight and then looked over at me. "There's something wrong with you, Izzie. I swear, there's something wrong with you."

"You've said that before. It's not true." I stood up, clutching the pillow to my breast. "There's nothing wrong with me. I'm just different from you, that's all. Different is not necessarily worse." I sped off down the stairs, leaving the box for her to lug. I didn't want to talk about Rob with her. I liked him. I liked him a lot. But I didn't love him; I couldn't love him. So maybe

Mimi was right. Maybe there was something wrong with me. But if there was, it was something I couldn't help.

Back in Winter Hill, we unloaded all the boxes into our cellar. I felt like Sisyphus, forever pushing his stone up a Hades hill, only to have it roll back down again. Mimi would repack and reorganize her boxes, and in another week those she was taking with her into her new life, plus all the wedding presents that had been falling in on us like snow for the past several months, would have to be carried out again to the post office to be shipped to Houston. In Winter Hill, however, the work went faster than it had in Philadelphia, because Pops and Faye helped too.

Afterward, Pops took us all out to supper. We were too tired to dress up for a real restaurant. We just washed our hands and faces and drove over to Donato's for pizza.

The five of us squeezed into a single booth, Pops and Faye on one side, with me on the other, sandwiched between Mimi, next to the wall, and Rob, on the aisle. Even though I knew the menu by heart, I examined the stained, faded card carefully, as if I expected to discover that by magic tempting, glamorous new items had appeared upon it. Fettucini alfredo, perhaps, or cannelloni, à la Mrs. Mangarelli.

"Well, folks, what'll it be?" I looked up when I heard the familiar voice of the waitress. But it wasn't

Kitty Fine who stood at the foot of the table. It was Marla. Kitty must have carried out her threat to find a better job, and Don must have hired Marla in her place.

"Hi, Marla," Rob said.

She stared at him sharply and then looked around at the rest of us, apparently realizing for the first time who we were.

"Hi, Marla," I echoed brightly. "You remember my parents, don't you, and my sister Mimi?"

They were paying customers. She had to say something. "Hello, Mr. and Mrs. Courtney. Hello, Mimi."

"It's nice to see you again, Marla," Faye responded cheerfully. "It's been a while."

"Has it?" Marla's eyes narrowed with suspicion.

"I was busy with my job, and now Marla's busy with hers," I interjected quickly. "We haven't had much time."

Marla allowed my explanation to stand. "So, anyway, folks, what'll it be?" was all that she said.

After we'd decided on our pizzas and our meatball sandwiches, and Marla had left to put in the order, I excused myself. "Sorry to bother you, Rob," I apologized, "but nature calls."

He stood up and let me pass. A few moments later, coming out of the rest room, I didn't return directly to the table. I went over to the counter where

Marla was getting our Cokes and beer. "Where'd Kitty go?" I inquired conversationally.

There was a long pause as she slowly pulled two cans of Bud from the refrigerator. But, finally, she answered me, and there was no anger in her voice. There was no emotion in it at all. "Kitty's working at the Ground Round out on the highway. A neighbor of hers works there too, so she has a ride."

"Well, I'm glad you got this job. Jobs are hard to find."

"You're telling me. What happened to yours?"

"I quit. I didn't want to. They made me."

"You mean your parents?"

"Yeah."

"Why?" The note of curious concern in her voice sounded almost genuine.

"They didn't like my boss. They thought he was after something."

She lifted her eyebrows. "Irresistible Izzie."

"I didn't think so," I replied tartly. "That's their idea. And it's nonsense."

"I don't really want to say this," Marla responded quietly, "but they may be right. Sunny told me where you were working. My grandmother lives in Denford. I've heard weird stories about that guy. He's really off the wall. You're better off not having anything to do with him." Her glance fell to the tray she was loading. "Rob is keeping you busy enough."

"Rob and I are just friends," I replied, my voice low. "You can believe that or not, as you choose, but it's true."

Once more she looked up at me. "I guess you can't help it, Izzie. I realize that now."

"Help what?"

She shook her head. "It doesn't matter. I'm glad you're not working for that old man anymore. Don't go back there."

I wanted to tell her that Leo was not an old man, but at the same time I didn't want to contradict her and thus perhaps ruin the beginning of the reconciliation that we seemed to be embarking on. As a compromise, I just sort of nodded.

"I'm going out with Eddie Soutine Sunday night," she volunteered. "I went out with him last Sunday too."

"Gee, that's great," I enthused. "He's a swell guy." I hardly knew him, but he'd always seemed nice enough.

"We can't go out Saturday nights," she said, "because I work Saturday nights."

"The trouble with this life," I said, "is that you either have time or you have money—never both at once."

"Listen, Don's giving me the eye. I won't have money anymore either if I don't get back to business." She picked up the tray. "It was good talking to you, Izzie. I'll see you around."

"Yeah, Marla, see you." I returned to the table, satisfied. We weren't exactly friends again, but we didn't seem to be enemies any longer either.

It was dark by the time Pops pulled his car into our garage. Pops, Faye, and Mimi called out their good nights and final thank yous as they entered the house through the back door. I walked Rob back out to his van, which he'd left parked at the curb.

I put my arm through his. "Rob, I can't thank you enough for all you're doing for us. Pops says you're a prince, and I know that Faye and Mimi feel the same."

He stopped in the middle of the driveway, turned so that he was facing me, and put both his hands on my shoulders. His elbows were bent; his head was only inches from mine. "I don't care what your parents think of me, or what Mimi thinks. I only care what you think. Do you agree? Am I a prince?"

Frightened by his intensity, I shivered and put my hands on his arms in an effort to release myself from his grip. But his fingers clutched my shoulders even harder so that we stood together for a moment, as if locked in a stiff embrace. "I like you, Rob. I like you very much," I whispered.

His hands left my shoulders, his arms went around me, and he pulled me to him. Then he bent his head and fastened his warm, firm mouth to mine. It happened so quickly I had no chance to protest. Deep inside of me, I felt a small leaf uncurl and reach itself forward, as if to the sun. I knew what it was; I didn't want it. I put my hands on his chest, pushing him away. "No," I said. "No. You said you wouldn't."

He dropped his arms and took a step backward. I could see his face, washed white in the moonlight, his eyes narrowed, deep lines etched at the corners of his mouth. "What does liking mean to you, Izzie?" he asked, and his voice, though low, was shot through with anger.

"I guess not the same thing as it means to you," I replied. I felt very sad.

"How long are you going to wait, Izzie?"

"I'm only seventeen."

"Only seventeen!" The sarcasm was thick in his voice. "Seventeen is not a child. It's time, Izzie—for something."

I shook my head.

"But I'm not the one, is that it?" His frown deepened.

If not him, then who? I couldn't imagine liking anyone better. So what was wrong? I didn't know; I couldn't explain. My finger rubbed nervously against the rose cameo ring on my finger. "Leo, it's not that—"

"My God," he protested, "now you can't even remember my name."

"What are you talking about?"

"Who the hell is Leo?"

"My boss at the florist shop. Remember? You drove me to his house that day."

Rob nodded slowly. "I remember. It's funny that you should call me by his name."

"Did I? I wasn't even aware I was doing it," I replied with a little laugh. "It was just a slip of the tongue. It doesn't mean anything. I must be getting like Pops. Sometimes when he wants me he has to call Faye and Mimi before he finally can get out 'Izzie.' When we had a cat, he had to go through her name too."

"Forget it, Izzie." He jerked his hand in an impatient gesture. "I'm sorry I mentioned it. I'm just going to go now."

I didn't really want him to do that either. "Listen," I reminded him, "I never promised you anything. You said you were patient."

"Yeah." He turned away from me. "Well, my patience has just run out. I told you I'd let you know when that happened. So it's happened." He took two long strides down the drive, and then he stopped and faced me again. I took a hesitant step toward him, but then I stopped too. "I'll be your date for the wedding, if you still want me to," he said. "I'll do all the driving I promised to do that weekend. I don't go back on my word. But that's all. After that, it's over."

"And until the weekend of the wedding?" There were still two whole weeks to live through until then.

"I won't be around. I won't see you in school either."

I took one more step toward him. "Can't we see each other sometimes? I'll miss you terribly. We've become such good friends."

"Geez, Izzie," he exclaimed, "I'm not made out of marble, like you. I'm only flesh and blood."

I turned and walked back to the house. He was being fair enough. He had kept his word. He had said he'd tell me when he'd lost patience, and now he had. There had been no promises between us, after all, no guarantees, no vows. Except for the one he'd seized a few minutes ago, not even any kisses.

But my heart was in my throat as I climbed up the front steps, and I was crying. For the second time in six weeks, I felt as if I'd lost my best friend.

I was angry too, so angry that I could feel my teeth clenching. Sex, that was the enemy. The movies and TV and all the magazine articles could rave on about it as much as they wanted, but I knew the truth. It was like a coil, wrapping around you, making a million connections you couldn't begin to straighten out. In one way or another, since the beginning of the year, it had been the ruination of the only relationships I cared about.

Eleven

I DIDN'T THINK I could sleep. Perhaps if I read a very good book, I would stop thinking about Rob, and Leo, who seemed to have gotten all mixed up together in my mind. I propped myself up against my pillows and began the first chapter of *The Return of the Native* by Thomas Hardy, which I should have finished a month ago for honors English but was just getting to now, a mere two weeks before the final exam.

The Return of the Native is, of course, a very good book. Everyone says so. I'm sure I'll think so too when I finally get around to reading it. But that night I was a lot more tired than I knew. I fell asleep with the light on, fully dressed, my watch still on my wrist, my little cameo rose ring still on my finger.

I slept deeply, but I dreamed. I know I dreamed, because in my dream I heard the phone ring, and that awakened me. I forgot what the dream was about almost as soon as I was awake enough to realize that the real phone in our real house was really ringing. But I didn't forget that I had been dreaming.

The phone must have rung a long time to impinge at last upon my consciousness, buried so deep in slumber. Fleetingly, as I got up to answer it, I wondered why it hadn't awakened anyone else. I glanced at my watch. It was three-twenty in the morning.

When I picked up the extension on the table in the upstairs hall, I heard the click that signifies a receiver being replaced in its cradle. Whoever it was, he had given up just as I had gotten there.

And then, suddenly, in a flash and with absolute certainty, I knew who had been on the other end of the wire. I seized the telephone again and pushed down the buttons for Leo's number. My fingers were trembling so that I kept making mistakes and had to dial three times. Finally, I got it right. I let the phone sound seventeen rings. I know, because I counted. No one answered.

I went back to bed. This time I undressed and shut out the light. But I left the cameo ring on my finger. I had made up my mind. That day, that very day, I was going to see Leo. I didn't care if Pops never spoke to me again. But I didn't think that would happen. He

170

would understand eventually. He had not brought me up to be the kind of person who abandons a friend in need. And if I knew anything that night, I knew that Leo needed me. It was a need born out of a despair that I had merely recognized but hadn't truly comprehended until that moment. Why then, and not before? Well, you don't know everything to start with. You have to learn as you go along.

I went out early, before anyone else was up, and clipped a blossom from the single rose bush in our yard. It was the only one that had opened, its deep red petals beginning to uncurl in the sun. I arranged it in a bud vase I had filled with water and placed it in the center of the table.

"Flowers for breakfast," Faye said when she came down and saw it. "How special." The four of us sat pleasantly together in the light-washed kitchen, eating the French toast I had prepared. "This whole breakfast is such a lovely treat before a busy day." Faye deeply appreciated any meal she didn't have to cook herself, no matter how elementary it was. "You must have been up with the sun."

"I didn't sleep so well after that phone call woke me about three-thirty."

"I didn't hear the phone ring," Pops said.

That was surprising. He was a light sleeper and usually heard everything.

"I didn't either," Faye said. "Did you, Mimi?"

She shook her head. "Who was it?" she asked.

"By the time I got there, the person had hung up."

"Probably a drunk somewhere, dialing the wrong number," Faye commented. "Who else would be calling us in the middle of the night? Maybe you just dreamt you heard the phone ring, Izzie."

I merely shrugged.

Mimi changed the subject. "You coming with us?" she asked. "We're going to the photographer's, and then to the caterer's, and then to the florist's. We've got to get them all in this morning." Needless to say, Mimi was not using Castle Florists for her wedding flowers.

"Not me," Pops said. "Paul Zeigendorf is picking me up in about half an hour for tennis, and then we're going out for lunch."

"You're not invited anyway," Faye retorted lightly. "You'd only get in the way."

"No more than Izzie," he protested, just as lightly.

"There's some truth to that," Mimi returned with a lazy smile.

"Well, you're safe, because I'm not coming either," I assured her. "Lucky you, all done with school—"

"Forever," she interjected joyfully.

"Yeah. But some of us poor plebians still have

exams coming up." I was trying hard not to actually lie. And truly I meant to tell them about seeing Leo— but afterward.

"Well, if you go to the library, don't forget to be back by one o'clock."

"I won't." Our final fitting for our dresses was at two at the bridal shop in Highland Park.

The three of them going out and leaving a car behind was a lucky break. It meant I didn't have to call a cab. This time, unlike last time, I couldn't count on Rob.

A little before ten, I pulled into the parking area next to Castle Florists, curiously deserted for a Saturday. When I reached the shop, I realized that the show windows were unlit. A crudely lettered sign had been taped to the door. It read

CONTACT NEW YORK OFFICE

followed by a phone number. I rattled the door, but it was locked, and peering through the window, I saw that the interior was dark and deserted.

I drove around the block, and parked on the street in front of the house. I tried the gate; it had been open when Rob had driven me over, but today it was locked. I left the car where it was, walked around to the shop again, and cut through the yard, the way I had done when I'd gone to the house for dinner all those times with Mr. Mahoney for chaperone. The hole in the hedge seemed to have grown together since I'd last used it, and I had to push the branches apart in order to get through. Sharp twigs pulled at my T-shirt and scratched my cheek. I wiped away a trickle of blood with a tissue and straightened my hair with my hands. I made my way through the garden, where clumps of weeds now clogged the path and the edges of the lawn grew ragged and unkempt. Though the spring blossoms were gone, for some reason, here the roses weren't out yet.

But I didn't linger in the garden. I moved quickly toward the house and climbed the front steps. The porch furniture was still under plastic covers, and the rhododendron bushes surrounding the building had grown so tall and thick that the porch was shrouded in gloom. Their purple blossoms were long gone, and the green of the their leaves was so deep it appeared almost black.

I rapped loudly with the knocker, three times, to make sure I was heard. Then I waited. I waited and waited. No one came. Again I lifted the knocker, and again, and yet again.

I pushed against the door, but it was locked, just as the gate had been, and the door to the shop. Though the day was sunny and warm, all the windows opening onto the porch were shut.

I ran down the steps and around to the back door. I'd never gone into the house through the back, but I'd seen the door and assumed it led into the kitchen or a pantry of some kind. I rapped at it several times, but still no one came. I stepped back and shouted. I called for Leo, for Mrs. Mangarelli, for Mr. Mahoney. It was as if I were shouting down a dry well. No one heard. Or if they heard, they chose to ignore it.

Perhaps someone I hadn't noticed was hanging about the shop. Maybe if I went back there and called and shouted and banged, I would raise a response. But I doubted it. So before I tried what I suspected would prove to be a final, hopeless gesture, I pushed against the back door with all my strength. It creaked, it shuddered, and then it opened.

There, standing not three feet from the door, was Mr. Mahoney.

"Mr. Mahoney," I cried accusingly, "why didn't you let me in? You heard me. You knew who it was. I bet you even saw me."

"Go away, Isabel," he replied, his eyes narrow and hard, his voice dead. "No one wants you here."

"I'll go away," I said, "as soon as I'm sure that Leo's all right."

"He's all right."

"I'd like to see that for myself."

"For God's sake," he shouted suddenly, his control breaking like glass, "haven't you done enough damage already?"

"He's sick, isn't he?"

175

Mr. Mahoney didn't reply. But I could tell from his eyes, wider now and filled with worry, that I was right.

"Don't you think," I said, "that before you send me away, you ought to ask him if he wants to see me?"

"So you'll see him," Mr. Mahoney said. "Then you'll go away again. And after that, he'll be worse."

Quickly, I moved past him. He reached out and grabbed my arm, holding it so tightly I couldn't move. Though well into his sixties, Mr. Mahoney had the grip of a young gorilla. "I only want to sit down," I assured him. "I've been standing out there for half an hour."

He let me go then, and I took a chair by the kitchen table. He remained on his feet, glaring at me.

I gazed up at him. "Just tell me what the matter is with him. Tell me what the doctor says."

His shoulders sagged. Slowly, he too pulled out a chair and sat down. "We haven't had the doctor," he whispered. "He won't let us call one."

"And you're listening to him?" I almost screeched. "What's the matter with you? Are you crazy?"

The deprecating wave of his hand seemed almost apologetic. "You know Leo."

"Well, then," I replied hopefully, "he can't be very sick."

"He's very sick."

"And you think that somehow that's my fault."

He stared at me without moving a muscle.

"Mr. Mahoney," I burst out, "I didn't ask him to love me."

"Then why didn't you go away?" he asked. "After that first time, why didn't you go away?"

Why indeed? Fear? Fascination? Greed? All of those things together? In the beginning, perhaps. But not later. "He had become my friend," I said quietly. "That's why."

"Then you should never have gone away at all," Mr. Mahoney said. "I'm not saying you had to love him the way he loved you. But you shouldn't have gone away. You should have loved him enough for that."

"I did. I do." But I didn't offer any excuses. They wouldn't have sounded particularly convincing, even to me. "So let me see him now."

He stood up. "Izzie, just go."

I rose too. The words I had to say to him had come to me at last. Looking directly at him, I spoke slowly and clearly, keeping my voice low and calm. "If you think my leaving is what made him sick, then regardless of what you think of me, your refusal to let me see him isn't helping him. He wants to see me, I know. If you keep us apart, then it's your own jealousy and your own spite that's at work, even if you might tell yourself that you're looking out for his best interests." I folded my arms across my chest and stood with shoulders back and chin up, staring at him.

Briefly, he returned my glance, and then his eyes fell away. "Come on then," he said gruffly. "Follow me."

He turned abruptly and left the kitchen. I trailed behind him, down the wide, tiled hall, always so brightly lit and full of flowers when I'd been there before, but today dim and smelling somehow musty and closed-up, like a house whose owners had gone off to Maine for the summer. We climbed the broad staircase to the second floor. Mr. Mahoney quickened his pace, and I had to hurry to keep up, fearful of losing him in the labyrinthine corridors of what was to me totally unfamiliar territory.

He stopped before a closed door, turned to me, and put his forefinger to his lips in what was a totally unnecessary gesture. Did he think I was going to march into Leo's room tooting a trumpet?

He stepped aside as he held the door open for me. I entered the room; he followed, and then shut the door. I wondered why. Mrs. Mangarelli was sitting in a straight chair by the bed. There was no one else in the house, I was sure.

The bed itself was a huge four-poster with a heavy, embroidered canopy above it. Thick, dark carpet covered the floor, and the crewelwork draperies, which matched the bed canopy, were drawn shut over the windows. The only sound was the whir of an ineffectual little electric fan atop an extremely tall chiffonier whose mirror seemed to scrape the ceiling. Tucked into the mirror frame was a newspaper clipping. I didn't have to get close enough to read it in order to recognize it, for I had a copy of it myself in my scrapbook. It was the article and picture of me that had appeared in the Winter Hill *Gazette*.

The room was so stuffy I could hardly breathe and so dim I could scarcely distinguish the outlines of the figure stretched out on the bed. I moved quietly across the floor, my feet sinking into the carpet with each step. Mr. Mahoney remained standing near the door. As I approached the bed, Mrs. Mangarelli stood up. I wondered briefly if she was as mad at me as Mr. Mahoney was. But the glance she bestowed on me as she approached was merely sad. "I suppose it's a good thing you've come," she whispered. "Not that it'll do any good. It's too late." She removed herself to another chair, near the window, allowing me to occupy the one next to the bed.

I pulled the chair closer and forced myself to look down at Leo, lying there on his back with his eyes shut and his arms stretched out on top of a light quilt that covered him to his chest. And when I looked, I felt no shiver of disgust. There was no room in my heart for disgust, it was so filled with pity and sorrow. If he was breathing, I could neither see nor hear it. His ravaged face was drained of color; his arms, in their short-sleeved pajamas, had lost all their flesh and muscle and had become nothing more than bones covered by a thin layer of wrinkled skin. His neck looked like a turkey's, with flaps of flesh sagging loosely. His fingers were the merest sticks.

I reached out and touched his forehead. It was dry and hot. Beneath his lashless lids, I thought I saw his eyeballs move.

I leaned over and said quietly, but in rather more than the whispers Mrs. Mangarelli and Mr. Mahoney seemed to favor, "Hello, Leo. It's me, Isabel." And then I touched his hand with mine.

The eyelids fluttered lightly a few times and opened. The eyes that stared up at me, which had once burned like black coals, were now dull and lifeless. But they saw. I knew that they saw. The lips moved and formed words I recognized, though I couldn't hear them. "Hello, Isabel."

"I'm going to give you some water, Leo," I replied matter-of-factly. "If you drink a little water, perhaps you'll be able to talk to me." He looked like a man who'd neither eaten nor drunk in a long time.

"He won't take any water," Mr. Mahoney said in a stage whisper. "He won't take anything. That's how this all started."

But Mrs. Mangarelli said, "There's a pitcher on the night stand. I've been wiping his lips with a cloth.

I'll get you a glass." She disappeared into the adjoining bathroom and returned almost immediately.

If Leo couldn't eat or drink, he belonged in the hospital where they could feed him intravenously. I supported his head and managed to pour a couple of drops of water down his throat. He swallowed them, whether willingly or not I couldn't tell. "Listen, Leo," I said, "what's this all about? Why did you let this happen to you?"

"No use. . . ." he murmured. "No use. . . ."

No use living, I suppose he meant. "No use to whom?" I exclaimed. "No use to Mrs. Mangarelli? No use to Mr. Mahoney?" Then I added firmly, "No use to me? You're not leaving, Leo. We need you." I grasped his hand and held it tight. "I'm calling the Rescue Squad. We're taking you to the hospital."

An angry spark brightened his lifeless eyes, and he shook his head with surprising violence.

"You see?" Mr. Mahoney said. He had moved away from the doorway and stood on the other side of the bed. "I told you so." He sounded almost complacent.

My eyes had been fixed on Leo, but I lifted my head now and looked at Mr. Mahoney. "You're angry at me, Mr. Mahoney? Well, I am very angry at you. He's in no condition to stop you from doing anything you want to do. How come you didn't send him to the hospital long ago?"

"I'm the boss," Leo said. This time I could hear him.

"No more you aren't," I retorted.

He seemed to collapse into his pillow, as if exhausted by the effort he had just expended. "Don't, Isabel. Not worth it." His voice was once again barely audible.

"I'll go with you, Leo," I said. "I won't leave you." I squeezed his hand, and then stood up.

"Leaving already," he accused in a hoarse whisper.

"I am not." I sat down again. "Mrs. Mangarelli, you call. You call the Rescue Squad. Is that OK, boss?"

He sighed, and I took it for assent. So did Mrs. Mangarelli. She dialed the phone on the night stand by the bed, and I heard her issue instructions in a low voice while I managed to get a little more water down Leo's throat. Then she called a doctor.

"Listen, Leo," I said. "Listen to me very carefully. I will always be your friend, always. And I am not the only one. You don't have to be alone. You don't have to buy friendship either. People would like you, if you would let them."

"The face . . ."

"An excuse. It can be fixed."

He shook his head. "Not worth it. Everybody goes away."

Don't risk loving, because the one you love may

fail you. My God, he and I were exactly alike. We were two sides of the same coin. Well, I had started to change. He could too.

I put my lips right to his ear. "Better to have loved and lost," I whispered, "than never to have loved at all."

"Terrible cliché," he muttered, but some of his old asperity was in his voice.

I leaned back. "True, nevertheless." I lifted his head again and held the water glass to his lips. I waited until he had swallowed twice, and then I said, "If you're better in a couple of weeks, you can come to my sister's wedding. That'll be a good place to start."

"You're crazy." He pushed my hand away, and water spilled out onto the bedsheet.

"Oh, Leo, now look what you've done." I wiped at the water with my free hand, and then I glanced as his face, resting now against the pillow. It seemed to me that I saw tears on his cheek. Or was it only a few more drops of water? "Mr. Mahoney," I ordered, "go down and wait for the ambulance so you can show the Rescue Squad the way up here. Mrs. Mangarelli, you better pack a little bag. Leo, you just rest."

"Boss?" That was Mr. Mahoney.

Leo nodded slightly, and then shut his eyes. Mr. Mahoney moved off to obey my instructions. "And leave the bedroom door open," I called after him. "We could use a little air in here."

I sat there, silently holding Leo's hand, while Mrs. Mangarelli bustled about throwing pajamas and toilet articles into a paper shopping bag. Even she didn't know where the long-unused suitcases were stored. In no more than five minutes, we heard the sirens of the ambulance as it came down the street. The Denford Rescue Squad was clearly a model of efficiency.

Of compassion too, for when it was clear to the two white-suited men who carried the stretcher and to the woman who came with them that Leo strongly resisted the idea of letting go of my hand, they allowed me to ride in the back of the ambulance with him. Mr. Mahoney followed in the Mercedes, but Mrs. Mangarelli remained at the house. She said she would come over to resume her vigil later. The circles under her eyes were deep and dark, and she didn't appear to have a great deal more meat on her bones than Leo. She was in desperate need of a little respite and a nap.

In the hospital, they took one look at Leo and sent him up to intensive care. He was dehydrated, according to Dr. Bettelheim. He was the one Mrs. Mangarelli had called. He had taken care of Leo years before when he'd had the accident. In another few days, Leo might well have been dead, Dr. Bettelheim said. He wasn't the first severely depressed person who'd simply stopped eating.

Mr. Mahoney and I were shown to a special waiting room that was part of the intensive care unit.

The nurse said that we could go in to see Leo, one at a time, for only five minutes out of every hour. And at that, they were making an exception, because we weren't even relatives. They were very strict in intensive care.

I left the door to the waiting room open and watched for the doctor. When I saw him hurry by, I rushed out into the corridor, calling his name.

He turned. "Oh, yes," he said. "Mr. Koenig's friend. He's all hooked up now. I think he's going to be all right. You got him here just in time. I must say, I can't understand why you waited so long to call me. But we can take that up later." He glanced at his watch. "I've got an office full of patients waiting for me. I'll be back later."

"Dr. Bettelheim, this situation is somewhat complicated. If Mr. Koenig doesn't see us, he may think we've . . . I've . . . deserted him," I tried to explain. "If he thinks that, he'll never get better."

Dr. Bettelheim put his hand on my shoulder. "My dear, I've known Mr. Koenig for a long time now. I told him you and Mr. Mahoney were in the waiting room. I told him you weren't going anyplace. I'll be back later this afternoon. If he responds to treatment, we'll get him out of intensive care in a few days." He lowered his voice. "When it's your turn to go in, stay a little longer. No one will notice."

Half an hour later, the nurse said one of us could

see him. I leaped to my feet. Mr. Mahoney, resigned, let me go.

The main area of the intensive care unit was a large room separated into small, three-sided cubicles surrounding a central nursing station. The cubicles were crowded, for, besides a bed, each contained various examples of the complex equipment of modern medicine. The curtain in front of Leo's cubicle was drawn. Even here, in ICU, where privacy was an unknown concept and everyone was presumed to have seen everything, Leo's appearance made him a special case.

The nurse pulled the curtain aside and gestured for me to enter. A bottle high on a rack dripped fluid down a long pipe into his veins. His eyes were shut, but already some color had returned to his face. His breathing seemed light, but regular.

I sat down next to him. "I'm here, Leo," I said.

He opened his eyes.

"I didn't leave."

"Dr. Bettelheim said you wouldn't. But I wasn't sure he was telling me the truth."

"I will have to go home eventually, but I'll come back tomorrow. Do you believe me, Leo? Then on Monday, I'll have to go to school. But I'll come in the afternoon. Do you believe me?"

He uttered a breathy little snort, a kind of substitute for a laugh. "It's all right, Isabel. You don't

186

have to ask 'Do you believe me?' after every remark."

"I'm going to stay until the nurse makes me leave. Dr. Bettelheim said I could. He's nice, and smart too, I think." I took Leo's hand. "Don't try to talk."

He nodded, and, with his hand still in mine, he shut his eyes. In just a moment or two, he seemed to have dozed off.

Perhaps I did too. I realized that a figure clad in green scrubs was standing in front of me, and I hadn't seen him enter the cubicle. "Oh," I thought, removing my hand from Leo's, "the doctor. He's come back sooner than he said he would." But when I looked up to confront the newcomer face-to-face, I realized that the man I was looking at was definitely not Dr. Bettelheim, or any other doctor, for that matter.

"Rob!" I exclaimed. "What are you doing here?"

"I might ask you the same thing," he replied. "Your mother and sister are mad as hornets. They went off to Highland Park without you. They sent me to look for you and drag you over there if I found you."

The fitting. I had forgotten about it, utterly and completely forgotten about it. "Oh, God," I muttered.

"You should at least have phoned."

Leo opened his eyes. "What's this?" he queried, his voice barely audible, yet containing in it more than a touch of his old authority.

Rob turned his attention to the figure in the bed for the first time since he'd entered the cubicle. "Hello,

Mr. Koenig," he said. "I'm afraid you don't look so good." He didn't avert his eyes.

"Rob!" I exclaimed again, this time in anger rather than surprise.

But Leo didn't seem to take offense. "Truer words were never spoken," he murmured. "Who are you anyway?"

"My name is Rob." The reply was in a voice almost as quiet as Leo's. "Robert Palowski." He paused as if waiting for some kind of response. When none came, he went on. "I'm a friend of Izzie's."

Leo's fingers closed tightly over the edge of the bedsheet. "What are you doing here? How did you ever get into ICU? Did you tell them you were my long lost sonny boy?"

"I . . . ah . . . well, I sort of borrowed these clothes from the linen room so I could pass for an orderly. I know they're strict."

"How enterprising. But why?"

"Well, I was looking for Izzie."

"For Isabel? Why?"

"Today's the final fitting for the dresses for her sister's wedding," Rob explained, taking a couple of steps toward the bed. "Her mother was frantic when she didn't get home in time to keep the appointment. She called me and asked me to go look for her. I had to leave work," he added, an aggrieved note creeping into his voice. "They couldn't send her father. He'd gone out to lunch with a friend, and no one knew where."

"How did you find me?" I wondered. "I mean, how could you even dream I'd be at the hospital?"

"Mr. Koenig's housekeeper told me."

"However did you come to her?"

"I went to the library first. I called Sunny, and Marla, and a couple of your other friends. And then I thought of Mr. Koenig. Remember last night?"

"What happened last night?" For a sick man, Leo sure was concentrating on the conversation.

"She called me Leo."

"By mistake," I interjected quickly.

"I knew you were on her mind, Mr. Koenig." He turned back to Leo. "So I drove over to your shop. And then when I saw that it was closed, I went around to the house. I saw one of the Courtneys' cars out in front. The gate was open, so I went to the door and knocked, and spoke to the housekeeper."

"You do put two and two together," Leo said.

"Yes," Rob replied. "And I always come up with four."

Leo's head turned on the pillow. "Very clever," he whispered. And then he shut his eyes.

"Rob, you better go," I interjected. "Leo is very tired."

"And you'd better come with me," Rob insisted.

"No," I protested. "I can't. Not yet."

Rob put his hand on the bed. "Mr. Koenig, I think Izzie has to go now. Her mother will kill me if I don't get her over to Highland Park right away. I'm afraid she's going to murder Izzie anyway."

Leo opened his eyes again. "Of course she must go. Just make sure she comes back tomorrow."

"Yes."

"Do you promise?"

Rob seemed a bit startled by that question, but decided to humor a sick man. "I promise."

"I promise too," I said. "Do you believe me?"

"Yes," he said. "I believe you." He turned his head a little so that he was facing me. "Isabel, will you kiss me good night?"

I leaned close to him. His whisper in my ear was barely audible. "Good night, Isabel."

I brushed his lipless mouth with mine. "Good night, Leo," I said. It wasn't night, but I said it anyway. "Good night. Sleep well."

Twelve

ROB BARELY GAVE ME a chance to poke my head in the waiting room to tell Mr. Mahoney I was leaving. "I'll be back tomorrow, Mr. Mahoney," I said. "Don't think I won't be."

"Why do you have to assure everyone half a dozen times that you'll be back tomorrow?" Rob asked as, his hand on my arm, he hurried me down the hall. "Why should they doubt it?"

"When I left—Mr. Mahoney thinks that's what made Leo sick," I explained.

"Does *he* think that?" Rob wondered. "Mr. Koenig?"

"Well, he does, partly. But partly he knows better."

We crossed the sun-drenched parking lot, heat rising in transparent waves from the asphalt. "I'll come back here with you tomorrow," Rob said.

"I thought you were through with me."

"I'm giving you another chance."

"At what?"

"We'll see."

He dropped me off in Denford, where I reported briefly to Mrs. Mangarelli, and then got in the car I'd left there earlier to drive on to Highland Park. Rob had to get back to work. "I'll come over to your house when I'm done," he said. "I have a feeling you're going to need me."

It wasn't until I got home that I understood what he meant. Faye and Mimi and the two bridesmaids who lived in the area were already long gone from the bridal shop by the time I showed up. Miss Edna and Miss Jane were extremely annoyed with me for arriving for a fitting two and a half hours late on one of the busiest Saturdays of the year. They said I'd have to wait, and wait I did, for over an hour, before the seamstress called me into the fitting room. It was after seven by the time I arrived back in Winter Hill, and I wasn't in the house five minutes before I wished I was still at Society Bridals. Compared to Faye and Mimi, Miss Edna and Miss Jane were teddy bears.

"That my own sister could be so incredibly inconsiderate," Mimi scolded. "It's simply beyond belief."

"Really, Mimi, no harm done," I dared to suggest. "My dress fits. It looks fine."

"If it weren't so late, I'd find another maid of honor," she snapped.

"You think that's some kind of terrible threat," I retorted. "Well, some things, just one or two things, are more important than your wedding."

"Like what?" Faye wanted to know.

"Like a friend in trouble," I said. "Like a friend who's sick."

"Why does everyone have to get sick right before my wedding?" Mimi moaned.

"Oh no!" I exclaimed. "Who else is sick?"

"Mrs. Darley's daughter," Faye replied with a gloomy shake of her head.

"Who's that?"

"Mrs. Darley is the florist. She had to fly out to Eugene, Oregon, to be with her daughter. I must say, when we stopped by there this morning, we weren't too impressed with the work her assistant was turning out."

"That's the understatement of the year," Mimi added with a grimace. "And then you messed up the fitting. Did you know we had a flat tire on the way home? It's been a wonderful day." She put both her hands to her head and ran all her fingers through her hair. "Really, Izzie, what friend could possibly be more important than your own sister?"

"Now, Mimi," Pops remonstrated, "let's hear

Izzie's explanation. If she was helping someone, that *is* important. She should have called, of course, but other than that—"

"Oh, cripes, Dad," Mimi groaned. "There you go again."

The doorbell rang, and with an enormous inward sigh of relief, I jumped up from the kitchen table. "I'll get it," I cried.

It was Rob. Prince Charming himself couldn't have been a more welcome sight, at least not to my eyes. "Too late?" he asked as he realized my distress.

"Just in time. We're only getting to the sticky part now."

He followed me into the kitchen. Faye was so intent on resuming our interrupted conversation she didn't offer him so much as a piece of fruit. "So who was this friend?" she asked. "It wasn't Rob, so who was it?"

"You don't even have any other friends," Mimi said. "Not any real ones."

"It was Leo Koenig," I replied quietly, ignoring her malice. "He was sick. I had to get him to the hospital."

"Izzie!" Pops exclaimed. "I forbade you—"

"I knew he was sick," I interrupted. "I just knew it. So I went over there. I was going to tell you."

"Were you?" His voice was cold and still.

"Yes, I was." I turned to him, holding his eyes

with mine. "He's my friend. There's nothing you can do about that. Pops, the way I left—that's part of what made him sick. I'm not blaming you for that. It's my fault. I shouldn' have allowed it to happen. It won't happen again."

"That's wh kept you from the fitting? Your old boss?" Mimi lifted her hands as if she were begging heaven for enlightenment. "That's who's more important than me—a monster."

I would not yell at her. I wouldn't. "He's not so bad. He's no monster."

"Oh, Izzie, how can you say that?" Pops shook his head violently. "I've seen him. I know what he looks like."

"Let me tell you, Mr. Courtney," Rob chimed in, "at this point he's as weak as a kitten. He couldn't hurt a fly." And then he added thoughtfully, "If he'd even want to. Which I don't think he would. I don't think you ought to hold his appearance against him. He's suffered enough on account of it. After a few minutes you more or less forget about it anyway."

It had taken me more than a few minutes. But, grateful for Rob's support, I kept that notion to myself. "If only you could really talk to him," I said. "Then you'd understand."

"I never want to lay eyes on that man again," Pops said.

"That's not important now," Mimi interrupted.

"What's important is this total lack of responsibility on Izzie's part."

"I promise I won't miss any more appointments," I assured her. I had heard that most brides go nuts right before the wedding, blowing up unimportant mishaps all out of proportion, and Mimi certainly wasn't proving an exception to the rule. It was too bad I'd made things worse instead of better.

With a great show of lifting his wrist and cocking his head, Rob looked at his watch. "Geez, it's nearly eight-thirty," he announced. "If we don't get out of here soon, Izzie and I'll be late for the movie. It goes on at nine. Can't you guys finish this discussion tomorrow?"

"Izzie, you never told me you were going to the movies with Rob tonight," Faye said. She almost smiled.

"I . . . I forgot. You know, it's not the only thing I forgot today." I almost smiled too, apologetically. I stood up. "Just wait a sec, Rob. I'll wash my face and put on a clean shirt." At the kitchen door I turned and faced them all. "Look, I'm sorry about today. But Leo is my friend, and he's sick. I will go on seeing him. I don't think you're going to throw me out of the house for that." I didn't wait for a reply, but continued on my way, trusting Rob to add whatever was necessary.

We didn't go to the movies. Rob said he needed

to talk to me, so we drove up to Rebel's Point and parked like all the other kids in the lot behind the overlook. Only they weren't talking.

"We can see the view better if we get out of the car," I said. "We can sit on a rock."

The night was mild, moonless, and studded with stars. The lights of the towns laid out in neat squares in the valley below us twinkled like stars too. "Stars above us and stars below us," I whispered. "It's wonderful, isn't it?"

"Yes," he replied quietly. "It's wonderful. Here, sit down." He had arranged himself on a flat, narrow shale outcropping. I sat down beside him. We were very close to each other, so close that our shoulders touched. I did not pull away.

A few moments passed in silence; the only sound was the light breeze rustling the leaves of the pin oak trees. Then he put his arm around me. "There's something I have to tell you, Izzie," he said. "About Mr. Koenig."

"I'm listening." My tongue was suddenly thick in my mouth, and I had difficulty forming the words.

"I know who he is."

"Of course you know who he is. We all know who he is."

"No, Izzie, only I know. And my parents. And I didn't know until today, when I learned his name." He squeezed my upper arm with his hand. "Remember,

I told you my sister was killed in an automobile accident?"

"Oh, my God!" I had made the connection in an instant. As I turned toward him, my face moved so close to his that even in the starlight I could see his eyes, wide and still. "Leo was driving the car. Your sister's name was Martha."

He nodded. "Martha Palowski."

"She liked being in plays," I intoned as if reciting a litany. "She was extremely beautiful. She was a little wild. More than a little."

His arm fell from my shoulder, and he turned his face toward the valley. "Yes. She looked something like you, I think. At least it seems so from the pictures. I never really noticed that until today."

"Does he know who you are? Leo, I mean."

"I don't know. I think I noticed him react when I said my name, but that doesn't mean he realizes I'm Martha's brother. There are plenty of Palowskis in the world. And he wouldn't even know Martha had a brother. My mother and father moved away from Denford right after the accident."

"What are you going to do?"

"Nothing. Except tell him. I have to tell him."

"I wonder how he'll react to that." Leo's hold on life was so fragile any blow could send him tumbling down the other side. Yet I realized I had no right to ask Rob to say nothing. "Could you wait until he's better?" I suggested hesitantly.

Rob put his hand on mine. "Izzie, I'm not planning to curse him out. I know who he is; I'm just going to tell him who I am, that's all. He didn't kill my sister on purpose. On the contrary, he tried to save her. He's been through hell too. Even my folks don't think about him anymore. They talk about Martha sometimes, but they talk about her alive, not dead. After a while you just have to get over things, if you're going to survive." His voice was low, but without hesitation. He had thought about all of this before. "I don't mean forget. I guess I mean forgive, or at least understand. Otherwise, you're dead inside. You're worse off than the dead person."

"Oh, Rob, how do you know so much?"

He took my chin in his hand and turned my face toward his. "Izzie, I think you know a lot now too."

And then I watched his face come closer and closer, as if in slow motion, or from a great distance away. I shut my eyes and felt the gentle pressure of his lips on mine. They were soft, and sweet, and sticky, like honey. I put my arms around him and pulled his body closer until I could feel it, pressed against me. Then his kiss grew harder and more insistent, and I was aware of every part of me, down to the deepest, most secret passages, unfolding, opening, waking up. I was aware even of my blood, throbbing through my veins.

After a while we stumbled back to the parking lot on shaky legs, giggling as we supported each other across the bumpy, stone-strewn hillside. In the van, though, I sat as far away from him as I possibly could. I needed to get myself back together. Besides, he was driving.

But in front of our house, we kissed again, and then we kissed some more. To me, each kiss was more delicious than the one that had preceded it. I didn't think I would ever get enough of them. It was Rob who said, finally, "I suppose you'd better go in, before your father comes out here with a shotgun."

"He's asleep," I murmured. I wasn't able to speak out loud. "Just a few minutes more." I smiled slowly. "I'm beginning to understand."

"Yeah," he returned dryly. "I guess you are." But he didn't kiss me again until, hand in hand, we'd walked up the path to the front door, and then it was only a peck on the cheek. "Tomorrow," he said. "Visiting hours begin at one. I'll pick you up a quarter of."

"And leave me alone all morning to deal with my family?" I protested, only half joking.

"A good night's rest should calm them down," he said. He squeezed my hand. "Sleep well, Isabel."

"You too, Rob." I stood on the stoop, watching until he and his van pulled away. Then I went inside, took a long, cool shower, and fell asleep, the excitement I could still feel lingering in my body defeated almost immediately by pure exhaustion.

*   *   *

In the morning I apologized to Faye and Mimi about five thousand times, and made no mention whatsoever of Leo until Rob came for me. Then I said we were going to visit him, together, and the fact that Rob was with me seemed to reconcile Faye and Pops to the inevitable, at least for the time being.

But Rob just dropped me off at the hospital, and came back for me later. He had decided to wait until Leo was out of ICU before seeing him again. It would be easier that way anyhow. He wouldn't have to steal any more scrubs from the laundry room.

Leo had improved remarkably in twenty-four hours. If a plant wilts from heat and dryness, and you remember to water it before it actually dies, you can almost see its leaves lift themselves up in front of your eyes. Leo was like that plant. All kinds of bottles still dripped their contents into his veins, but his eyes were open and he was listening to chamber music on the radio when I walked into his little cubicle.

"Isabel," he said. "You remembered."

"You knew I would." I sat down in the chair next to his bed.

"Yes, I knew." He managed a kind of smile. "Where's your chum?"

"Who?"

"The boy. Robert. Robert Palowski. He said he was coming too."

I wondered if Leo had guessed. "He thought he'd better wait until you were in a regular room. He didn't want to press his luck." I wanted to change the subject. "Let me fix your pillows. They're all wrinkled." I rose from the chair and spent a little time fussing with Leo's bedclothes. When I had arranged things to suit both of us, I sat down again. We talked for a while, and then I read to him from a trade magazine Mr. Mahoney had brought over. Leo wasn't quite up to reading for himself yet.

I came back the following day after school, by myself. They'd pulled out the tubes and were feeding him puddings and soft-boiled eggs and other mushy things by mouth. He didn't ask after Rob again. We talked about a lot of different things. After all, we had never lacked for conversation. One of the topics we discussed was the wedding. I didn't bring up the idea of his coming, but managed to make a fairly amusing story out of all of poor Mimi's disasters over the weekend. Leo enjoyed most of it, except that he didn't find Mrs. Darley's incompetent assistant very funny. I should have known he wouldn't.

Wednesday afternoon they moved him out of intensive care and into a private room. Friday Rob came with me to the hospital. All week, when I wasn't in school, I'd spent my time visiting Leo and running errands for the wedding. Rob had spent his time working. We'd both been studying for exams. We'd been so busy that it was the first we'd had a moment alone together in days. The elevator we rode was large, empty, and very slow. We didn't waste any time. We kissed all the way up to the fourth floor, arriving flushed and breathless.

"We have to stop meeting like this," Rob whispered in my ear as we hurried down the corridor, his arm around my shoulder, his head bent toward mine.

I giggled as he kissed my ear. But in front of Leo's room he dropped his arm. I smoothed my hair and preceded him through the door.

The nurse had cranked up Leo's bed before we arrived and had combed his thick mane of hair. Instead of one of those horrible puke green hospital gowns, he was wearing his own monogrammed silk pajamas, and he looked almost human.

"What an improvement," I said as I sat down on the end of the bed. Rob took the chair.

Leo regarded me for a long, silent moment. "And you are looking even more ravishing than usual," he said at last.

"Thank you. We can attribute that to the rapid progress of your recuperation."

"Not entirely—if at all." He glanced over at Rob. "As for you, Mr. Robert Palowski, you look like a cat with an empty bowl in front of him and cream all over his whiskers."

"I feel pretty good," Rob allowed modestly.

"Do you mind if I ask you a few questions?" In typical Leo fashion, though he worded his remark like a request, he was actually making a statement.

"Shoot."

"Do you have any brothers or sisters?"

So Leo did know, or at least he suspected. Rob didn't seem surprised at the question, for his reply was immediate and straightforward. "Not now. But my parents had another child. A girl. She died before I was born. Her name was Martha."

A long breath of air passed through Leo's mouth like the sound of a dying wind in autumn.

"She was killed in a car crash," Rob said. His voice held no rancor, and his face was without expression. "You were driving."

"Oh, my God!" Leo exclaimed, his hand jerking up to cover his eyes. "I knew it. I knew it when I heard your name. What are you going to do?"

It was the same question I had asked.

"I'm certainly not going to pull out a gun and shoot you, Mr. Koenig. You didn't want Martha to die."

"But it was my fault. Her death was my fault."

"She pulled at your arm," I cried. "So in a way it was hers too."

Rob nodded. "Dad told me that part. You must have told the police, and they told him."

"He's forgiven me? Your father's forgiven me?"

Leo dropped his hand and looked at Rob, his voice as eager as a child's.

"Forgiven? I don't know. He's let go, I guess. That's what he's done. My mother too. They live a very full life . . . a very good life. . . ."

"They've recovered."

"People do. More or less."

That was what he had told me, twice. My eyes moved from his face to Leo's.

"See that?" I said.

"Do you think there's a resemblance between Izzie and my sister?" Rob queried bluntly.

"Yes, I do," Leo admitted.

"Well, I don't," Rob snapped. Saturday night at Rebel Point he'd thought so too. Now, for some reason, he had changed his mind. "They're nothing alike. I don't think Martha was a pleasant person. I mean she was pretty and talented and smart, but she was spoiled and selfish too. Of course, Mom and Dad would never say that. But I've gathered as much from other relatives, old family friends—"

"Nobody's perfect," Leo offered, almost angrily. "She never had the chance to grow up. She might have changed as she matured."

"Maybe," Rob said. "Maybe not." He stared directly into Leo's eyes. "I'm probably nicer than she ever was. I *know* Izzie is."

"I've improved recently," I murmured.

"You ought to let go too, Mr. Koenig," Rob said. "You ought to have some plastic surgery and try starting over."

"Rob!" I cried. "Don't. That's none of your business."

"I'm right," Rob insisted. "He knows I'm right."

"I don't know anything of the sort!" Leo exclaimed. "I do know that you're one fresh kid." I was relieved. Leo annoyed was a big improvement over Leo sad. "I think you should get the hell out of here," he added.

"OK," Rob said, standing up. "But I'm coming back tomorrow. So long, Mr. Koenig. See you later, Izzie." His tone was actually jaunty. He seemed quite pleased with his afternoon's work.

I didn't stay much longer myself after Rob had left. He'd been gone only a few minutes when Mrs. Mangarelli appeared at the door. She said that Dilly was downstairs waiting for the other visitor's pass. They only issued two for each room. "It's OK," I said. "I'll go. I've been here long enough."

"But you're coming back tomorrow?"

"Of course." He asked me that every day.

"Both of you?"

"You mean Rob?"

"Who else?"

"He said he was coming. Are you sure you want him to?"

Leo nodded.

"That's not just more of your self-torture, is it?" I asked softly.

Leo snorted—or laughed. I wasn't sure which. "I was a fresh kid myself once," he said.

I didn't think Rob was fresh, exactly. That is, I didn't think so any longer. He was supremely confident, that's what he was. It came from having known, right from the day he was born, that he was the crown prince of the universe—at least so far as his mother and father were concerned.

I kissed Leo good-bye and left. In the corridor, I encountered Dr. Bettelheim. "Hi, Isabel," he said. We'd run into each other almost every day that week. "How's our patient this afternoon?"

"Dr. Bettelheim, there's something I've been meaning to ask you." I didn't want to bring the subject up again with Leo, or mention it at home, until I'd checked it out with the doctor. "Is there any chance that Leo will be out of the hospital by next Sunday?"

"What's next Sunday?" Dr. Bettelheim returned.

"My sister's wedding. I'd like him to come."

"A public appearance, huh?" He raised his eyebrows. "He's made a lot of progress in the last few days, but I'm not sure he's ready for that. It might even trigger a setback. Let's not kid ourselves. Even the most compassionate among us, or the most blasé, does a doubletake at the sight of Leo Koenig."

Except, for some reason, Rob. But Dr. Bettel-heim was essentially correct, of course. "Look, Isabel," he said, "I don't know if Leo will be out of here in a week. In a way, I hope he isn't. I hope by then I've talked him into beginning the plastic surgery. But if he is, then he's a free man. He can go where he pleases."

I nodded. There was no point in urging Leo to come until I'd taken it up at home. I'd wait awhile to see what happened.

Thirteen

I BROACHED THE SUBJECT of Leo and the wedding on
Saturday night when Rob came to the house to pick
me up. Mimi played right into my hands. "You have
to wear a suit next Sunday," she warned him. "I hope
you have one."

"Don't worry, Mimi," he assured her, grinning.
"I won't shame you. I've been to weddings. I know
how to act. I promise not to kiss Izzie in public—only
you. I'm allowed to kiss the bride, aren't I?"

"Yes, you are," Mimi replied primly. "On the
cheek."

"I'd like to bring someone else to the wedding,"
I announced mildly. "In addition to Rob, that is."

"Who?" Mimi asked.

"Leo Koenig. If he's better by then. If it's OK with you."

"It certainly isn't OK," Pops interjected. "Isn't it enough that you run to see him at the hospital every day?"

"He can't come to my wedding," Mimi said in a tone of utter disgust. "He'd ruin it."

"Don't be ridiculous, Mimi," I cried. "How could he ruin it? No one will be looking at him. They'll be looking at you."

"Anyway, he's going to have plastic surgery," Rob announced confidently.

I glanced at Rob, surprised. How did he know that?

"Not by a week from tomorrow, he isn't," Faye responded grimly.

"It would be so good for him to come," I said. "It's just what he needs—to be among people and see that they don't drop dead at the sight of him."

"Look, Izzie." Mimi's fists were clenched in her effort to achieve a reasonable tone of voice. "Let's forget everything else. Let's forget what Mr. Koenig needs. Let's forget what you need. Let's just remember that we're talking about *my* wedding." Suddenly her control broke, and she nearly shouted. "Not about a therapy session."

Well, it was Mimi's wedding, not mine. I couldn't bring someone to it without her permission.

"But I'm not giving up," I told Rob after we had left the house. "I'll just wait until she's in a good mood to mention it—if she ever is again, before the wedding."

"I think she'll start cheering up by the middle of the week," Rob suggested, "once Neil arrives and things are really underway."

"Yeah," I said. "Good idea. I'll wait till Neil gets here. And you can talk to Leo. You seem to have the inside track with him now. He never said anything to me about plastic surgery."

"Well, he hasn't exactly consented to it yet. I just bring it up every time I see him."

I shook my head. "Boy, you sure have nerve. I didn't realize you were seeing him other times too. I mean, when I'm not there."

"Just for a few minutes, now and then."

"Like every day."

He shrugged. "You bring up the plastic surgery too," he said. "No one else means more to him than you, Izzie. That's still the truth."

The next week was the most hectic I'd ever experienced. After Monday, I never got over to the hospital at all. Rob did, though, and issued brief reports when we met. We were never alone but saw each other amidst an ever-increasing aggregate of relatives. Maybe it was just as well that we had a few days to kind of cool down. Where we were going after the wedding was over was something we'd have to work out. Once upon a time lovers in fairy tales got married and lived happily ever after, even if they were only seventeen. It's more complicated nowadays. I suppose it was always more complicated, in real life.

On the actual morning of the wedding, however, Pops, Faye, Mimi, and I sat quietly in the sun-drenched kitchen and ate toast and drank coffee together. Pops had insisted on that. "Just the four of us, for the last time," he said. Neil had been staying with us since he'd come up from Houston on Wednesday, but that last night, after the rehearsal dinner, Pops made him go to the motel with his parents.

Mimi had protested, but, surprisingly, Faye supported Pops. "It isn't appropriate for the groom to sleep in the same house as the bride the night before the wedding. You'll see him tomorrow morning, in the church. That's time enough."

"For heaven's sake, Mother," Mimi cried. "Don't be so medieval. The days of the virgin bride are gone forever."

"You wanted the white gown, Mimi, and the champagne, and the flowers, and all the other traditional trimmings. This one comes with the package."

"You're throwing Neil out," she complained. "I think that's ghastly."

"No, it's all right," Neil assured her, smiling. He whispered something in her ear, and then she smiled too.

And the next morning, wrapped in a faded chenille robe that she'd received as a fourteenth birthday gift and hadn't packed because she was at last abandoning it, she appeared as cool and collected and beautiful as she did nearly every other day of the year. The nerves she'd exhibited earlier had dissipated with Neil's arrival, just as Rob had predicted, though I had never found just the right time to bring Leo up again.

Now the moment was upon us. There was no point any longer in worrying about the clothes or the flowers or anything else. What would be would be, and both Mimi and Faye were smart enough to accept that. Mimi poured cream into her coffee and said, "This was a good idea, Pops. I'm glad you insisted."

He kissed her cheek. "An island of quiet, before the day goes wild." Just then, the doorbell rang. "See what I mean? And it isn't even eight o'clock yet." He left to answer it. A few moments later we heard the sound of something heavy being dragged along the front hall. And then, through the kitchen door, came a blooming rose bush in a great earthenware pot. Behind it, his face the same color as the roses from the exertion of pushing it, came Pops.

He stood up and wiped his forehead with his sweatshirt sleeve. "That man delivered it," he said. "That man who works for your Leo Koenig."

"Mr. Mahoney," I said.

"He wouldn't come in," Pops added. "I asked him. I asked him if he wanted a cup of coffee."

213

I noticed a little white card dangling from one of the branches. I crossed the kitchen, picked it up, and read it out loud. "To all the Courtneys, but especially to Mimi. A precursor of things to come. Happy Wedding! Leo Koenig."

I looked from Mimi to Pops. He shook his head silently. I looked back at Mimi again. "And you wouldn't even let him do your wedding flowers," I said.

"It's magnificent," Mimi breathed. "Too bad there's no way of getting it to Houston. I guess it'll just have to stay here. I never saw a bush like it. What kind of roses are they?"

"I don't know the name," I said, "but I recognize the blossoms." They were pink, shading from a pale yellowish tint in the center to a deep rich color on the edges.

Pops nodded. "It's the same bush I picked the rose from that day I went there. I knew it wouldn't die."

In all the weeks I'd worked at Castle Florists, I'd never seen it. I wondered where Leo had hidden it.

Pops settled the rose bush beneath the kitchen window, and we finished our breakfast while inhaling its sweetness. Now I was sorrier than ever that Leo wasn't coming to the wedding, and I wondered if Faye and Pops and Mimi weren't just a little bit sorry too.

But in the end, Leo did come.

Not that we saw him when we first arrived at

the church. He wasn't there, though I recognized his influence as soon as I walked in. It took the others a little while to figure out what had happened. Masses of greens had been banked in back of the altar and along the walls. Scattered among them were baskets of pink and yellow roses. Posts had been placed at intervals along the center aisle, and atop each one, more rose baskets turned our plain little old church into a royal bower. Mrs. Darley's assistant, a thin young man named Alvin, with small eyes and big ears, was tying a wide white ribbon into a bow around one of the posts. The others were already similarly decorated.

"Alvin!" Faye exclaimed. "What's going on here?"

His narrow underlip quivered. "I thought you'd like it."

"It's goregous. But we can't afford it."

His look of bewilderment was pitiful. "Some people came from Castle Florists—you know, over in Denford—"

"Yes," Pops said, "we know."

"They said they were going to help me, no charge, because they said Mrs. Darley had helped their boss when he was in trouble. I mean, I . . . I didn't ask too many questions . . . I was kind of glad. This was a big job." He had been in over his head. Faye and Mimi had recognized that two weeks ago. "Do you think they went too far?" he added, his eyes darting from one exquisite bouquet to another.

"No," Mimi said firmly, "they didn't. It's magnificent. We're very happy. Thank you very much, Alvin. Where are all those people from Castle Florists? I'd like to thank them too."

"Oh," said Alvin, "they're gone."

She turned to me. "A precursor of things to come," she murmured.

We heard the crunch of automobile tires on gravel. Cars were pulling into the parking lot; the rest of the wedding party was arriving. Soon the guests would be coming too. There was no time to stand staring in amazement at the transformed church, and not even time to talk about what had happened. With the bridesmaids we retreated to the minister's office where we fussed with our makeup, smoothed our dresses, arranged Mimi's veil, and posed again and again for the photographer.

And then, at last, all the guests were seated The wedding party gathered in the vestibule of the church. The organ struck up Purcell's "Trumpets Voluntary," the doors were thrown open, and two of the ushers unrolled a long white velvet runner down the center aisle. Our minister, Mr. Ingleberry, was already stationed at the altar. His eyes were bright, and he was almost smiling. He wasn't much older than Neil, and he loved doing weddings. I guess most ministers do. They're a lot more fun than some of their other duties.

Neil's mother and father went down the aisle first, and sat in the front row. Neil's friend Ernie escorted Faye, smiling and glowingly beautiful in her dress of mauve chiffon. She sat in the pew directly across the aisle from Mr. and Mrs. Hammond. Then the two other ushers, in pale gray morning suits with pink roses —ordinary pink roses, supplied by Alvin—in their buttonholes, marched down side by side. They stationed themselves next to Ernie on the steps leading up to the altar. After that, Neil came, accompanied by his brother Stu, his face serious but composed, white lilies of the valley pinned to his lapel. They stood at the altar, facing the minister, their broad gray-clad backs straight and still.

Our cousin Estelle, Stu's wife, and Mimi's best friend from college were the three bridesmaids. They wore gowns of lilac cotton batiste and carried sheaves of long-stemmed pink roses. They glided along the white runner, one by one, and took their places on the steps opposite the ushers.

Then I came down the aisle. My gown was a deeper color, almost purple, and I carried long-stemmed pink roses too, mixed with some white ones. I moved slowly, as I had been instructed, eyes fixed in front of me, smiling slightly.

When I reached the altar, the music changed. The

organist struck up the wedding march from *Lohengrin* and I, like everyone else in the church, had eyes only for Mimi, coming down the aisle on my father's arm, her free hand holding a Bible decorated with a spray of white roses and orchids. Her full-skirted silk gown, with its scooped neck and puffed sleeves gathered in just above the elbow, appeared to have been designed just for her. Even beneath her veil, we could see that her face shone like a madonna's.

They paused just before they reached the steps. Pops lifted her veil, kissed her, let it drop again, and seated himself next to Faye. Neil walked down the steps, took the arm Pops had released, and led Mimi to her place before the minister.

They recited their vows, not only the ancient ones from the prayer book, but the special, personal ones they had written themselves. I lifted Mimi's veil and held her Bible while they exchanged rings. Mr. Ingleberry spoke of the sacredness of the covenant into which they were entering, and then he blessed them. He pronounced them husband and wife. The triumphant notes of Mendelssohn's "Wedding March" filled the church as Neil took my sister in his arms and kissed her.

In the order opposite that in which we'd slowly and solemnly made our way up the aisle, we flew down it again, all coupled now, and grinning so broadly that the people watching might have thought our cheeks were going to crack. It was all right. They were all grinning too.

Exultant. That was the only word to describe the way I felt. I hadn't known in advance that I would feel that way. I had never suspected.

And it was not until then that I saw Leo. He was sitting in the very last row, next to Rob, dressed in one of his dark, impeccably tailored suits, now much too big for him, with a broad-brimmed hat shadowing his face. I lifted my hand and waved, and smiled. Both he and Rob waved back. He raised his head, and for a moment I saw his features, clear and unshadowed. I knew that if he could have smiled, he would have.

And then he was gone. On the lush green lawn in front of the church, beneath the perfectly cloudless blue of the sky, we stood in a line to receive the guests. Rob was the last, and he was alone. He gave me a real kiss on the lips, not one of those polite cheek pecks considered appropriate on such occasions. Obviously, not only had he forgotten his promise to Mimi, he also didn't care if he smeared my makeup. Neither did I.

"I never kissed you while you were wearing lipstick before," he said. "Tasty."

I looked past him. "Where's Leo?"

"Mr. Mahoney drove him back to the hospital. Dr. Bettelheim had only given him a two-hour pass. He made me and Mr. Mahoney promise on our lives to get him back. Now that Leo's agreed to the plastic

219

surgery, Dr. Bettelheim would like to chain him to the bed so he can't run away." He took my arm and led me in the direction of the table where the punch bowl and trays of cold hors d'oeuvres had been set out.

"Did you know he was going to send all those flowers?"

Rob nodded. "I promised him I wouldn't tell. He was afraid someone would say no if he offered ahead of time."

"I wish he'd stayed just long enough for us to tell him thanks," I said.

"He took a big step today," Rob replied quietly. "It was enough for the first time."

I nodded a reluctant agreement.

"It's all right with him," Rob said.

"With Leo?"

"Yes."

"What's all right with Leo?"

"Us."

"Rob, what do you mean?"

"We have his permission."

I paused beneath a huge oak tree that had been growing for a couple of hundred years, long before the church, or the lawn, or the town of Winter Hill were even dreamt of. "He said that? How dare he?"

"Not in so many words." Rob stood still at my side. "But I know it."

"We don't need his permission."

"Maybe not. But he thinks we do."

"I hope, one day, he'll be happy," I said.

"Yeah," Rob replied in what was almost a whisper. "I hope so too."

Under the broad sweep of the oak tree's low, spreading branches, we were alone for a moment, in the coolness and the shade. Gently, Rob took me in his arms. We kissed, a long, sweet kiss, and then, hand in hand, we rejoined the wedding.

Barbara Cohen

is a well-known author of novels and stories for young people, including the classic *The Carp in the Bathtub*. Among her popular novels are ALA Notable Book *Thank You, Jackie Robinson*, *Bitter Herbs and Honey*, *The Innkeeper's Daughter*, *Queen for a Day*, and the award-winning *King of the Seventh Grade*. She is also the author of *I Am Joseph*, an ALA Notable Book, and *The Binding of Isaac*, both illustrated by Charles Mikolaycak; *Yussel's Prayer*, also an ALA Notable Book; and *Molly's Pilgrim*, with pictures by Michael J. Deraney; as well as *Gooseberries to Oranges*, an ALA Notable Book, and *Here Come the Purim Players!* both illustrated by Beverly Brodsky.